RETURN TO BLACK BEAR MOUNTAIN

HARDY BOYS ADVENTURES™

#20 *RETURN TO BLACK BEAR MOUNTAIN*

FRANKLIN W. DIXON

ALADDIN   New York London Toronto Sydney New Delhi

ALADDIN

An imprint of Simon & Schuster Children's Publishing Division

1230 Avenue of the Americas, New York, NY 10020

First Aladdin hardcover edition February 2020

Text copyright © 2020 by Simon & Schuster, Inc.

Jacket illustration copyright © 2020 by Kevin Keele

THE HARDY BOYS MYSTERY SERIES, HARDY BOYS ADVENTURES, and related logos are trademarks of Simon & Schuster, Inc.

Also available in an Aladdin paperback edition.

All rights reserved, including the right of reproduction in whole or in part in any form.

ALADDIN and related logo are registered trademarks of Simon & Schuster, Inc.

For information about special discounts for bulk purchases, please contact Simon & Schuster Special Sales at 1-866-506-1949 or business@simonandschuster.com.

The Simon & Schuster Speakers Bureau can bring authors to your live event. For more information or to book an event contact the Simon & Schuster Speakers Bureau at 1-866-248-3049 or visit our website at www.simonspeakers.com.

Series designed by Karin Paprocki

Jacket designed by Tiara Iandiorio

Interior designed by Mike Rosamilia

The text of this book was set in Adobe Carlson Pro.

Manufactured in the United States of America 0120 FFG

2 4 6 8 10 9 7 5 3 1

Library of Congress Cataloging-in-Publication Data

Names: Dixon, Franklin W., author

Title: Return to Black Bear Mountain / by Franklin W. Dixon.

Description: First Aladdin hardcover/paperback edition. | New York : Aladdin, [2020] | Series: Hardy boys adventures ; book 20 | Summary: Brother detectives Frank and Joe return to dangerous Black Bear Mountain to help locate a scientist gone missing from a remote research station. |

Identifiers: LCCN 2019019140 (print) | LCCN 2019021722 (eBook) | ISBN 9781534441347 (eBook) | ISBN 9781534441323 (pbk) | ISBN 9781534441330 (hc)

Subjects: | CYAC: Mystery and detective stories. | Brothers—Fiction. | Mountains—Fiction. | Wilderness areas—Fiction. | Missing persons—Fiction.

Classification: LCC PZ7.D644 (eBook) | LCC PZ7.D644 Rem 2020 (print) | DDC [Fic]—dc23

LC record available at https://lccn.loc.gov/2019019140

CONTENTS

RETURN TO BLACK BEAR MOUNTAIN

GRAVE RUBBERS

1

JOE

IT'S NOT EVERY DAY YOU GET A LETTER FROM a notorious convict asking for help locating a scientist who's gone missing from a remote mountaintop research station. In fact, my brother Frank and I were probably the only people ever to get one. I figured we were definitely the only ones to ever read said letter in a two-hundred-year-old country graveyard.

I yawned away some of the sleepiness from our bumpy sunrise bus ride to the mountains, adjusted my seat in the grass to get comfortable against the mossy old headstone I was using as a backrest, and pulled the letter from my pack. I could practically hear the author's deep voice and thick Russian accent in my head as I reread the opening paragraph aloud.

"'I know is inconvenient for the young detectives, but if you would go please to see the doctor to make sure everything is okay. I have heard not from him at all for too long after he wrote me very worried letter about unscrupulous people skulking in the old neighborhood.'"

I studied the hastily scrawled handwriting, hoping it might reveal new information to help us on our expedition.

It had been over a year since we'd last seen Aleksei Orlov, the fugitive mobster-turned-feared-hermit-turned-selfless-hero who gave up his own freedom to help us on our previous death-defying trip to Black Bear Mountain. When Aleksei wrote *the old neighborhood*, I had no doubt he meant the top of the mountain—where he'd faked his death and hidden from authorities for decades while pretending to be a mythical man-eating mountain man to scare people away. Including us. I'd been convinced he wanted to turn me into supper right up until the moment he saved my life.

Usually when I thought of Aleksei and his off-the-wall stunts, it made me smile. His letter from federal prison did the opposite.

"I hope Dr. K is all right and just out in the field doing research somewhere," Frank commented. The identity of the "doctor" in Aleksei's letter wasn't hard to guess either, and he wasn't a medical doctor. Renowned scientist Dr. Max Kroopnik had been the only other person besides Aleksei to make his home on Black Bear Mountain. "Aleksei wouldn't have been so cryptic in his letter and asked us to come all the way out here if he wasn't really concerned, though."

The early morning sun lit up the sheet of paper Frank had taped to a particularly ancient headstone to hold it in place while he made a rubbing of the dead guy's name with a fat black crayon.

"I wonder if there's secret information he didn't want the prison censors to see," Frank's ex-girlfriend Jones added as Frank handed her the finished paper. "Ooh, good one, Frank. Alistair Fritwell, 1691 to 1747. This is the oldest yet. It's perfect for my project."

Jones had convinced Frank that making grave rubbings for her school project on colonial life in the Northeast wilderness was a good way for us to kill time while we waited for the general store across the street to open. That was where we planned to catch a ride for the next leg of our trip. Our car was in the shop, so Frank and I had taken the early bus to the tiny mountain town of Last Chance, about two hours away from our hometown of Bayport. It was the last stop before you hit the high peaks, which loomed over the town in the distance. Our final destination—Black Bear Mountain—loomed the tallest.

At this hour, nothing in the town was open yet—not that there was much, just a handful of shops and a couple of restaurants. Which was why we were hanging out in a graveyard. Well, that and Jones's school project.

"I enjoy hanging out in creepy old cemeteries as much as

the next horror movie fan, but messing with graves like that gives me the willies," I said. My body gave an involuntary shiver to prove it. Jones was homeschooled by her mom, so her homework tended to be more nontraditional than ours. A lot weirder, too, apparently.

"We're not messing with them, Joe. We're making a historical record to preserve them," Jones said as she started in on a large headstone with a spooktacular-looking angel on top.

"Better grave rubbing than grave robbing, that's what I always say," Frank added cheerfully. "Besides, you're the person who's using someone's grave as a lounge chair."

"Thanks for sharing, Karl," I said to the occupant under my lounge chair as I scanned ahead in the letter for additional clues to our friend Dr. K's apparent disappearance.

Yup, just another day in the life of the world's greatest teenage detectives.

"Can you read the rest of the letter again, Joe?" asked Jones, which kinda irked me a little, if I'm being totally honest.

This wasn't the first time she'd tagged along on one of our investigations. She'd proven herself to be a pretty good detective, too, I had to admit. She'd even saved my tail on one occasion. The only problem was that when she tagged along with us, I was the one who ended up feeling like I was tagging along with *them*. The Hardy boys had always been a detective duo, and I wasn't thrilled about

4

Jones turning it into a trio—or feeling like the third wheel in my own outfit.

Jones wasn't Frank's ex because they didn't still like each other. All you had to do was see them making googly eyes at each other from behind their tombstones to figure that part out. They'd probably still be making googly eyes at each other all over Bayport, too, if Jones's mom hadn't gummed up the works for them by moving away. They'd stayed good friends, though, and she now lived closer to Black Bear Mountain than we did. So when Frank told her where we were going, she jumped at the chance to join us and took a bus to meet us here. Which, I had to remind myself as I gritted my teeth, made Frank happy *and* might actually help us solve the case—and Joe Hardy isn't the type of guy to get in the way of his brother's happiness or an investigation.

So I un-gritted my teeth, cleared my throat, and did as Jones asked.

"*In final letter to me, Doc say new scientist named Drawes muscling in on research territory and wanting to take mountain lion grant funding for himself. He say this man's research methods are suspect. Not very good scientist. I think maybe is clue for boys.*

"*Doc sends me letter here every five or six weeks to remind me of home so I do not miss it as much while I am away, but I do not receive one for too long now.*

Doc is very thoughtful friend. He would not forget about Aleksei. I fear is my fault if something happen to him. You find Doc for Aleksei, yes?

"Your friend for always, the Heroic Hermit of Black Bear Mountain."

"I like this guy," Jones declared.

"We do too," I agreed, smiling at the nickname he had given himself at the end of our last adventure together.

"So you guys told me about the bears, but there are mountain lions here too?" Jones asked apprehensively.

Black bears living on Black Bear Mountain wasn't a huge surprise, and we'd had a couple of close calls with them on our last trip, but mountain lions were a new twist. I'd be lying if I said I wasn't a little apprehensive about it myself. A little excited, too. I wasn't as into the nature and science stuff as Frank, but the prospect of seeing a real mountain lion in the wild had the adventure bug in me psyched.

"Historically, this was always mountain lion country, but they were hunted virtually to extinction in the northeast nearly a hundred years ago," Frank informed us, going into junior scientist mode. Dr. K would be proud. "There have been a number of reported sightings in recent years, though, and Dr. K was able to document evidence that two adults have been active in this mountain range! He and some other scientists believe that small, isolated populations of escaped captives and migrated individuals from out west are reestablishing themselves. He's been trying to capture and fit them with radio collars to study their behavior. If he can prove to the scientific community that there's a viable breeding population, it would be a huge ecological victory."

"Bringing back large keystone carnivores can help restore an ecosystem's natural predator-prey equilibrium by controlling overpopulated species, helping to regulate everything from vegetation health to disease-carrying pests like ticks," I added casually, earning a raised eyebrow from Frank. "You're not the only one who pays attention in science class, bro."

"Don't mountain lions have huge territories, though?" Jones asked. "That's got to be really challenging research."

"Yup, they're super-elusive, solitary creatures, and there may be only a few of them in the whole region," Frank confirmed. "The average person could spend years in mountain lion territory and never catch so much as a glimpse. Most people don't go off searching for them like Dr. K does, though. If we're lucky, Aleksei is worrying over nothing, and he's just away from the mountaintop tracking them."

"That's what the rangers thought when we contacted them to see if they could check on him. They've got their hands full anyway. Their buckets too." I pointed to the thick gray smoke rising from the mountain range north of Black Bear Mountain. There was a dark cloud over our expedition, and it wasn't just concern for our friend Max. "That forest fire has all their resources tied up."

The morning sunlight took on a strange orange glow

from the fire. It was kind of beautiful, but also really eerie. You could smell the smoke in the air from miles away. Not ideal hiking conditions, for sure, and we wouldn't have risked it normally, but making sure Dr. Kroopnik was safe took priority.

"It doesn't help that Dr. K is so hard to reach," Frank said. "There's still no cell service on Black Bear Mountain, and the only way to reach his research station is shortwave radio."

"And the doc isn't answering," I added. "So that means it's up to us to go find him."

We'd promised to come back to Black Bear Mountain to visit Dr. K and Aleksei after Aleksei was released from a prison in a few months, but this trip wasn't the vacation we'd hoped for.

The alarm on Frank's watch beeped. "Time to get moving. The general store should be opening and we can get the shuttle out to the Bear Foot Lodge."

"I can't wait to see the lodge," Jones said as she rolled up the gravestone rubbings she and Frank had made. "From everything you've told me about it, it seems like an amazing place."

"It sure is. Too bad we won't be there for long, though," Frank replied. "With a little luck, we'll find Dr. K, and be able to get back there to enjoy it before heading home in a couple days."

The Bear Foot Lodge wilderness retreat had been the launching point for our last adventure to Black Bear Mountain and would be again this time. Black Bear Mountain was about as remote as it gets, and the lodge made the perfect home base to set out from. They were even providing us with a wilderness guide to take us into the backcountry and up to the research station. The reason we'd arrived in Last Chance so early was to give us time to make the trek to the top of the mountain while it was still light out. If everything went well, we'd be waving hi to Dr. K before the sun set that night.

We shouldered our hiking packs, stepped through the wrought-iron cemetery gate, and headed across the street toward a large, hand-painted sign that read:

LAST CHANCE GENERAL STORE

GOODS · GIFTS · TAXIDERMY · BUS STATION

POST OFFICE

"With a town this small, I guess it's good to multitask," Frank observed.

We stopped in front of the glass window to look at the display of hiking and fishing gear, souvenirs, and dead animals. Yup. Dead animals. Lots of them. A fox chased a rabbit past a pyramid of honey jars on one end. Hats and fishing lures dangled from the antlers of a white-tailed deer on the other. A skunk perched on a mannequin's shoulder in the center. And a turkey swooped above them all with a salami gripped in its talons.

"It's creepy, if you ask me," Jones said.

"Little bit," I agreed.

The sign on the door flipped from CLOSED to OPEN and the door swung open with a jingle.

"Welcome and good morning!" a middle-aged man with sandy hair and a wispy mustache greeted us from the doorway. "You must be the famous Hardy boys. Everyone was talking about you after your last visit to the area. Quite the hullabaloo that stirred up. Folks will be telling their kids about it for ages."

"Ooh, I didn't know I was traveling with celebrities," Jones teased, giving Frank a playful nudge, causing him to blush and me to roll my eyes.

"And you must be Jones," the man said. "The Bear Foot Lodge called ahead yesterday to reserve our shuttle service for the three of you. We run the most reliable shuttle service in the whole area. We also happen to run the *only* shuttle service in the whole area." He gave a good-natured laugh. "Come in! Come in!" He held the door open as we walked into the store.

"I'm Ken Fritwell, by the way, proud proprietor of Last Chance General—the first and last stop for just about anything you could ever need in Last Chance. Whatever it is, there's a good chance we sell it, supply it, stuff it, shuttle it, or ship it."

"Fritwell? Are you related to the Fritwells that are buried in the cemetery?" asked Frank.

"Ah, I see you stopped across the street and paid a visit

to ol' Uncle Alistair," Ken guffawed. "There have been Fritwells living in Last Chance since before it was founded. We used to run the whole town back in the good old days. Times are a little harder here than they used to be, but no one knows these hills better than a Fritwell."

He paused to straighten one of the displays. "If you'll excuse me for a minute, my wife, Cherry, and I are still getting set up for the day. Give us a few and we'll get you in the van and on your way to the lodge. Why don't you three leave your packs at the front of the store, while I bring the van around and load everything up? We'll get you on your way to the lodge in just a few minutes."

"That would be great. Thanks, Mr. Fritwell," Frank said.

"Ken," he replied with a click of his tongue and a friendly finger gun in Frank's direction. "Take a gander around the shop while you wait and see if anything strikes your fancy. We've got some great camping gear on sale and all kinds of souvenirs for the folks back home."

We left our packs by the door and ventured into the store. Looking around, we quickly discovered that the inside of the Last Chance General Store was just as weird as the outside. Mounted taxidermy animals everywhere—some of them dressed in human clothes. I had to agree with Jones. Creepy.

A lifelike raccoon seemed to stare at me from a shelf full of packages of trail mix. The raccoon wasn't exactly appetizing, but the trail mix made my stomach growl and reminded me I reminded me that all I'd had to eat since we'd gotten on the bus was a handful of grapes and a dry energy bar. Thoughts of macadamia nuts, dried cherries, and dark chocolate danced in my head as I reached for the bag.

That's when the raccoon shrieked and leaped straight at my face.

ZOMBIE 2

FRANK

MY HEAD SNAPPED AROUND AT THE overlapping sounds of a wild animal shrieking and my brother screaming.

"Zombie raccoon!" Joe wailed as the animal leaped off the shelf, snatched the bag of trail mix from my brother's hand, and ran off down the aisle carrying the bag in its mouth, chittering in a high-pitched voice as it went. I could see a bald patch the size of a softball on the raccoon's rear end.

"Ricky!" a woman's voice yelled. "Leave the customers alone!"

A tall, middle-aged woman in denim overalls with a long ponytail draped over her shoulder stepped out from behind the counter. The raccoon dashed up her leg like she was a human tree trunk and climbed onto her shoulder, where it started to tear the bag of trail mix open with its dexterous little paws. It gave a little hiss as she grabbed the bag from it.

"Give me that," she tsked. "Bad raccoon."

With the trail mix gone, the animal started to chew on the woman's hair instead.

"Oh, stop that. Go to your bed," she ordered.

The raccoon gave another hiss, but it miraculously obeyed, running back down her body and scurrying over to a little dog bed in the corner, where it curled up and started chewing feverishly on a squeaky toy.

"Um, that thing's not stuffed," Joe said, his voice cracking.

"Not yet. He will be if he keeps this up. Sorry about that. I'm Cherry, the other half of Last Chance General," Ken's wife said, combing the raccoon tangle from her hair.

Jones looked back and forth from the raccoon to Cherry with a mix of shock and amusement. "You keep a wild animal as a pet?"

Cherry grinned. "If you ever get it in your head to adopt a baby raccoon, think twice. Oh, sure, they start out all cute and lovable, but they're just miserable teenagers. Nothing against teenagers, mind you. You're not all bad, and most of you outgrow your rotten phases, unlike our Ricky here."

Ricky the Raccoon looked up from his chew toy and chattered at her.

"Oh, hush, mister. You know it's true." She gave the raccoon a scolding look, but she also had a little smirk on her lips. "He's actually a pretty good companion when he's not causing trouble. Smart as a whip. We named him Ricky on account of the chittering he makes sounds a lot like *rick-rick-rick-rick*."

"It really does," I said. "There's a word for that—"

"Onomatopoeia," Jones interjected. "When a word mimics the sound it describes. Beat you to it, Frank."

I could feel my cheeks flush as she smiled at me. Jones and I might just be friends now, but she still kinda made my heart melt.

"How did you come to adopt him?" she asked Cherry.

"Our friends Steven and Dan out at Bear Foot Lodge found him in the woods," Cherry replied.

"We know Steven," Joe said coolly.

I didn't know who Dan was, but we definitely knew Steven—because he'd aided and abetted Lana, the woman who'd kidnapped Dr. K and nearly tossed Joe off a bridge while trying to cash in on the reward for Aleksei's capture and steal a stash of rare gems he'd been hiding. They'd been doing it to help Steven's wife, Casey, save the lodge from going under, but their good intentions had gotten out of hand pretty quickly, as they often do when crime is involved. Lana, Casey's sister, had been the one who'd caused the real harm, and she was serving time in prison because of it. Steven had basically just covered for her, and he got off with a slap on the wrist from both the criminal justice system and Casey, who'd been devastated. But

Casey was just as warm and forgiving a person as she was a wonderful lodge keeper.

Steven had been super apologetic to us too. He and Casey were both out of town this time, but when I'd called the other day about us coming, he'd insisted on comping us for as long as we wanted to stay. They were even providing the wilderness guide for free.

"Well, some scoundrel went and shot poor little Ricky in the keister with bird shot," Cherry continued, not seeming to notice the chill in Joe's voice. "He was just a tiny thing, but he had a big heart. Steven and Dan nursed him back to health—well, everything except that bald patch on his butt. But Casey didn't want him running around the lodge causing a ruckus with their guests, so—"

"So now he's running around our store causing a ruckus with ours," Ken cut in jovially, stepping back into the store from outside. "The van is parked out front now, so you can get on the road whenever you're ready, Cherr."

"Thanks, hon." She planted a kiss on his cheek. "We're just suckers for helpless things in need. No kids of our own, you know."

"With Ricky, we've gone from helpless to help *us*," Ken said. "Every now and then we send him out to the lodge for a playdate with Steven and Dan to give us a break from raccoon-rearing."

Ken nodded at the stuffed bear key chain Jones had picked out before Ricky stole Joe's trail mix. "Nice choice, young lady. The bears are always a favorite. Step on up to the counter and I'll ring you up."

"It's for my mom. I always bring her back a little something when I go away from home," Jones said, setting the key chain on the counter.

"Hey, it's Commander Gonzo!" Joe exclaimed, pointing to the wall beside the counter.

The kooky bush pilot who had flown us from Bear Foot Lodge to Black Bear Mountain on our last trip stared back at us from a poster advertising his charter plane business. That flight had been both the shortest and the most hair-raising plane ride of my life.

"That guy's really a pilot?" Jones asked, staring dubiously at the picture of the goofball in the battered floppy hat, oversize yellow aviator glasses, and impossibly tacky floral Hawaiian shirt. He was grinning ear to ear while giving the camera the double thumbs-up from the cockpit of his small Cessna airplane. Below that, the poster read, SKY-HIGH CHARTERS BY RETIRED USAF FLIGHT COMMANDER D. "GONZO" GONZALES.

"Gonzo may be a bit eccentric, but he's the best bush pilot in the whole region," Cherry said proudly.

"Also the most terrifying," I added. "He's a super-nice guy, and he flew back up to rescue our friends when they were stranded. I'm just not sure his grasp on reality is the tightest. He almost crashed just for kicks, and that was *before* we even took off. He told us his old squadron nicknamed him Doc Gonzo because he spent so much time in the infirmary recovering after wrecks. Everyone on board thought we were done for."

"Eh, you say 'terrifying,' I say 'exciting,'" Joe countered.

"The Commander is out of state on a charter assignment for corporate clients for the next couple weeks," Ken explained.

We'd tried calling him after we received Aleksei's letter and got a recorded message saying the same thing. Gonzo being gone-zo may have been the best thing for my nerves, but it definitely complicated the expedition. The flight from the lodge had taken only a few minutes. Traversing the backcountry on the ground and hiking in was going to be an intensive, all-day affair. We'd tried a couple of other local charter outfits, but they'd been booked solid.

As Ken handed Jones her change and a small paper bag with her key chain, a souvenir mug filled with pens next to the register caught my eye. It read, I SURVIVED THE WILD MAN OF BLACK BEAR MOUNTAIN in bloodred letters with a drawing of a maniacal-looking, wild-bearded hermit based on the legend Aleksei had fostered for himself to scare people away.

"Big seller, that one," Ken said, seeing my glance. "We've got T-shirts and tote bags too. This is another popular one."

He pulled out a hoodie that said BLACK BEAR MOUNTAIN on the front and HERMITS, MOBSTERS & BEARS, OH MY! on the back.

Cherry gave the sweatshirt one of the same *tsk*s she'd given to Ricky earlier. "I think it's just scandalous they're letting that scary mobster out of prison so soon."

"He's really not that scary once you get to know him," I told her.

"I probably wouldn't even be alive it weren't for Aleksei," Joe said. "If it had been up to me, he wouldn't have gone to prison at all."

It was actually in part thanks to us that he hadn't had to go away for longer. I'd figured out that the statute of limitations had run out on most of his crimes, and we'd even provided affidavits about his heroism to his defense attorney so he could plead for leniency with the judge. It helped that Aleksei was truly remorseful for what he'd done: with Dr. Kroopnik's help, he'd sold a fortune in super-rare demantoid green garnets over the years and anonymously donated all the money to his victims. Because his crimes were so old and none of them were violent, the judge agreed to a short sentence in a minimum-security prison as punishment for faking his own death so other fugitives wouldn't get the same idea.

"I never got the chance to meet Mr. Orlov, but I'm grateful to him for helping my boyfr—I mean my friends," Jones said, blushing a little as she corrected herself before continuing, which made me blush and made Joe roll his eyes again. "I think sometimes people can do bad things and still be good people if they take responsibility for their actions and try to make things right. He even turned himself in to help people who needed him. I'm proud of Frank and Joe for standing up for him, even though it wasn't popular with everyone."

"Well, I don't know about all that," Cherry said skeptically. "I'll be in the van when you're ready."

As she headed for the door, Ricky hopped up to follow her, jumping up on the counter and grabbing a piece of beef jerky out of Joe's hand on his way out the door.

"Hey! That's mine!" Joe protested.

Ken sighed and shook his head. "That raccoon eats more of our inventory than anyone in town." He picked a fresh stick of jerky out of a bin on the counter and handed it to Joe. "On the house. You have to understand, that whole ordeal with your mobster hermit friend frightened a lot of folks around here."

"From all the souvenirs with the Wild Man on it, I'd say it's been pretty good for business, too," Joe pointed out.

"I gotta admit, it has been recently. That cannibal hermit legend scared a lot of visitors away from the area for a long time, though. All the press your adventure and Orlov's arrest got thankfully changed that overnight. Lots of outdoors-lovers got to see how beautiful it is up here from all the pictures in the news, not to mention all the lookie-loo tourist types that make the trip just to see where all the scandal happened. And almost everyone who goes out there stops here first, since Last Chance is the last stop before you hit the wilderness."

All those tourists might be good for the town's economy, but they weren't necessarily good for the woods or Dr. K. Not all hikers and campers were responsible when it came to leaving the woods as pristine as they'd found them, and they might even be getting in the way of Dr. K's research. Could he have gotten into a fight with one of them?

"Speaking of hitting the wilderness, we'd better get going," Joe said. "We've got a long day of trekking ahead of us, and we don't want to lose too much daylight."

"Have a safe trip!" Ken called as we headed for the door. I could hear him talking cheerfully to himself behind the counter as we left. "Hmm, maybe we can get Orlov to pose for pictures and sign some of our Wild Hermit T-shirts when he gets out."

Well, if nothing else, Aleksei's ordeal had opened up a whole new tourist trade for the tiny town of Last Chance.

"I'm sorry if I seemed a little testy back there," Cherry said with a sheepish smile as we climbed into the back of a passenger van with the words LAST CHANCE GENERAL—MOUNTAIN SHUTTLE emblazoned on the side. "I didn't mean to talk badly about your friend. It just upsets me a little knowing there was a real-life criminal hiding in our own backyard, scaring people for all those years."

Ricky chittered in what seemed like agreement from a child seat in the passenger seat next to Cherry. He was even strapped in with a seat belt like a little furry kid.

"It's understandable that you were frightened, but Aleksei really is a good guy," I said. "He's looking forward to coming back and showing everyone he can be a valuable member of the community."

Cherry didn't look convinced, but she smiled anyway.

"Oh, I almost forgot! I've got something for you before we hit the road. Just a little token to say thanks for your business and apologize for Ricky terrorizing you all like that." She handed Joe a braided camouflage bracelet with a small compass built into the clasp. "Last one we had left in stock, so you'll have to share. It's made of the same kind of paracord the special forces use. Virtually unbreakable. Get yourself in a pinch, just unbraid it and use it as rope. And the compass'll make sure you always know which way you're going."

"That's awesome, Cherry. Thanks." Joe snapped the bracelet onto his wrist. "Pretty snazzy."

"So you and Ken haven't heard from Dr. Kroopnik at all for almost two months?" I asked. I'd asked Ken over the phone when we booked the shuttle as well, but it's always good to be thorough.

"Not a peep. Max usually flies his chopper down every five or six weeks or so to stock up on supplies, pick up his mail, and drop off honey for us."

"Honey?" Joe asked. Of course my brother was interested in the food part of it.

"Oh, yeah, he's quite the beekeeper, and his hives make

just the most exquisite honeycomb. Max says it's something to with the pollen from the fancy rare flowers up there on Black Bear Mountain. I don't know about all that science stuff, but wow, is that honey good. The customers love it. Flies off the shelf as soon as he drops it off."

I was pretty sure Cherry meant the indigenous Siberian flowers from the seeds Aleksei brought with him to make his mountain hideout feel more like his childhood homeland.

"The fancy flowers you're talking about are probably the native Ural Mountain species Aleksei planted," I informed her.

Cherry smiled at us in the rearview mirror. "Well, see there, I guess I do have something to be thankful to your Mr. Orlov for."

It was nice to hear we were winning new friends for Aleksei, but it was Dr. K I was really worried about. "No one's gone up there looking for Dr. Kroopnik to see if he's okay?"

"Nah. Max keeps his own schedule," Cherry said casually. "Not unusual for him to wander off into the woods for weeks at a time for some science-y reason or another. Wish he'd hurry up and get back from wherever he is, though, because we've been out of his honey for weeks, and the regulars are getting ornery about it."

"What about the new scientist who's been doing research on Black Bear Mountain, Drawes?" asked Joe.

"Humph, that city slicker," Cherry replied disdainfully.

"Now Max Kroopnik may not be a local, but he's been living out here for a few years now and does all he can to support our little economy. Buys all the supplies he can from us, even the stuff that costs more than it would if he ordered from those blasted big-box stores who like to undercut all the little guys 'n' gals. Drawes? That cheapskate drives in all his own supplies and has the rest shipped in off the Internet. Only time he bothers with us is to use the post, but he won't drop a penny in the shop or any of the other local businesses, for that matter. The way he looks down his nose at the locals, you can pretty much hear him calling us hillbillies in his head."

"Has Dr. Kroopnik said anything about him?" Jones asked.

"Oh, Max doesn't like the fellow any better than we do," she confirmed. "Said he thinks Drawes may even have sabotaged some of his experiments."

Jones, Joe, and I shared a concerned look. Aleksei's letter had implied something similar. I'd done some online research on Drawes before our trip, and the results weren't encouraging.

"He's published a few articles attacking the methodology of Dr. Kroopnik's mountain lion research," I shared. "That kind of vocal criticism can be really damaging. There are limited grants available to fund scientific research like this, and competition for them is fierce."

"Is it fierce enough to take out a rival?" Jones asked.

"Because that's what it sounds like this Drawes guy is to your friend Dr. Kroopnik."

Jones's question lingered in the air. If a person was willing to resort to sabotage to get ahead of the competition, what else might they be capable of?

"Come to think of it, poor Max seems to be getting into all kinds of squabbles lately," Cherry said, grabbing our attention again. "Been lots of tension between him and the folks at the lodge, too, ever since that stunt Casey's sister pulled, tying him up and stealing his identity the way she did when you boys were here last. Don't think Max ever forgave Steven for letting it happen. Doesn't help that Steven is fly-fishing buddies with Drawes either. Sad to see friends fall out like that."

The three of us did a retake of our concerned look. That was two people who had bad blood with Dr. Kroopnik, and they both knew each other. When I looked out the window, I could see a dark cloud of smoke rising into the sky beyond Black Bear Mountain like a bad omen.

VIP TREATMENT

3

JOE

I'S A GOOD THING THAT FOREST FIRE IS ON the other side of the river, north of Black Bear Mountain," Cherry said, wrinkling her forehead at the smoke rising over the next mountain range. "The air quality's been none too good, but the rangers say so long as the weather holds like it's supposed to, it isn't a threat to Black Bear or the valleys this side of the mountain."

The river ran down Black Bear Mountain through a large valley a few miles below where the lodge is. I'd flown it in a helicopter with Aleksei, so I knew it well.

"I wonder what Dr. K thinks about the wildfires as a scientist—assuming he's okay." Frank paused and bit his lip before continuing. "Fires like the ones out west can be devastating, but in some circumstances, periodic or controlled burns can be a natural, and even healthy, event in an ecosystem's life cycle—"

"Yeah, when they're controlled or natural," I said, interrupting Frank. "According to the news, the rangers think this one could have been set by a person."

"Why would anyone start a forest fire?" Jones asked incredulously.

"Probably just some careless campers," Cherry speculated. "Lots of the city folks who come up here don't know a lick about campfire safety or how to take care of a campsite. They start their weenie roasts willy-nilly without worrying about what's around them, leave the embers burning when they're done without dousing them, and don't think twice about tossing cigarette butts in a pile of dry leaves."

Cherry grew angrier as she spoke, and I didn't blame her. I love nature and take my responsibility to help care for it seriously. Our first trip to Black Bear Mountain to see Dr. K had even been with the Bayport High environmental conservation club. But even if you're just visiting the outdoors to have fun, responsible hikers and campers live by the motto "Leave it better than you found it." Because if we don't take care of the natural world around us now, it won't be around for us to enjoy later.

Even with the smoke and the eerie light it caused, the place was mind-blowingly beautiful. There were farmhouses along the way, but most of the trip was all woods and wild-life. The rest of our shuttle ride passed in a blur of gorgeous mountain scenery—and Ricky's raccoon snores. Yes, raccoons snore! And it's loud!

"Good luck, kids. I'll be back with the van in three days for the return trip home," Cherry chirped as we unloaded our gear from the van a little while later. "I'd normally stick around for a glass of the lodge's homegrown herbal sun tea, but Ricky and I have to get back to the shop to help out Ken. Stay safe, ya hear?!"

"Rick-rick-rick-rick," added Ricky.

The three of us took in the rustic log cabin wilderness lodge, surrounded by beautiful mountains and a ton of awesome outdoor activities, from zip lines to white-water rafting to horseback riding. Bear Foot Lodge looked like it had gotten a bunch of expensive new upgrades since we'd been there last too.

"Whoa, this place is amazing!" Jones said as the van pulled away.

"We like to think so," chimed the pretty young woman with short blond hair and rosy cheeks now standing the lodge's doorway. She was carrying a tray with three tall, frosty glasses of iced tea and, from the delicious smell of them, fresh-baked oatmeal raisin cookies. "Welcome to the woods. I'm Casey's cousin, Amina, the new assistant inn-keeper. You can leave your bags on the porch for now and grab some refreshments. Dan will bring them in."

"Don't mind if I do, thanks," I said, dropping my bag and grabbing a glass of tea in one hand and a warm cookie in the other. "This cookie is delicious!"

Amina smiled. "Fresh out of the oven just for y'all. Casey was super bummed she couldn't be here to greet you herself."

"This tea is amazing. What is that, hibiscus and mint?" Jones asked.

"Two kinds of wild mint, actually, along with passion-flower, borage, and a bunch of other edible flowers and herbs from the garden. All picked fresh and sun-brewed right here at the lodge," Amina replied proudly. "It's sweetened with honey from our own beehives."

"There's a whole lot of beekeeping going on up here, huh?" I asked. "Cherry told us that Dr. K kept his own hives to make honey too."

Amina nodded. "It's definitely a popular pastime out here in the woods."

"An important one too," Frank said. "Bee populations are declining drastically, and they're one of the most important pollinators that we rely on for global food crops. It's weird to think about, but without bees, a lot of the world could go hungry!"

"Spoken like a true beekeeper," Amina said. "Come on in and I'll show you to your rooms. You've got the best views in the whole lodge. Oh, and Casey said not to even think about trying to pay for anything while you're here. You boys are Bear Foot Lodge VIPs for life."

I guess almost getting killed solving a mystery while staying at the lodge had its perks.

"That's really nice of her, but I don't think we're going to need the rooms right now," Frank said apologetically. "We're actually kind of in a hurry to get up to Black Bear Mountain and set up camp while it's still light out."

Amina frowned. "We've all heard so much about the Hardy boys, the new staff was really looking forward to getting to know you. I guess you're eager to go looking for the treasure, though, huh?"

Frank and I both did a double take.

"Treasure?" we asked at the same time.

"Well, yeah. Casey and Steven don't talk much about that part of it, because of, well, you know . . ." Amina cut herself off.

We did. I could imagine Casey's sister going to prison for crimes she committed with Steven's help wasn't a popular topic of conversation around the lodge.

"But everyone knows about what happened from all the news reports and everything," Amina continued. "The headlines got a ton of publicity for the lodge. It totally turned things around. There aren't many guests here now 'cause of the fire, but we're usually booked solid. I even heard Casey say your heroics put Bear Foot Lodge on the map and practically saved us from going under."

"Um, you were saying something about a treasure?" Frank muttered, trying to change the topic back to something more relevant.

"Oh, yeah, well, the news reported all about the Wild Man having a fortune in rare green garnets."

"But Aleksei's garnets were lost in the river," I interjected. Casey's sister had lost the demantoids after falling in while trying to escape. I didn't mention what Aleksei had secretly hinted to Frank, Dr. K, and me afterward, though.

Amina looked around and lowered her voice to a whisper. "Sure, that's what the news said he *claimed*, but there were all kinds of rumors online that he secretly hid a whole other stash of them somewhere on Black Bear Mountain."

I winced and Frank did the same—because that's exactly what Aleksei had privately hinted to us. There wasn't any public evidence of it, but I wasn't surprised there were rumors. The mere mention of the word "treasure" makes people's imaginations run wild, and the only proof anyone had that the demantoid garnets were all lost was Aleksei's word for it—and Aleksei's mobster rep didn't make him seem like the most reliable source.

"No one's found them yet," continued Amina excitedly. "But we've had treasure hunters booking trips to go searching for them ever since. One of them checked out a few days ago, right after you called to book your rooms."

I saw Frank's face fall and knew exactly why. The news stories had identified Dr. Kroopnik as both a kidnapping victim *and* Aleksei's friend. That meant that any treasure hunter who went searching for the garnets on Black Bear Mountain might think Dr. K knew where they were too. And that made him a target.

"Amina, can you tell us—" My question was cut off by a pained moan from Jones.

"Frank," she croaked in a hoarse voice. "I don't feel right."

I heard Amina gasp as I turned to look at Jones. I'd thought treasure hunters were going to be the most alarming surprise of our arrival at Bear Foot Lodge. I was wrong. It was the angry red hives rapidly spreading across Jones's grotesquely swollen face.

ALL FALL DOWN

4

FRANK

ALL IT TOOK WAS THE SOUND OF Jones's voice for me to know something was wrong. Seriously wrong.

When I'd glanced at her a minute ago, she'd been fine. But now her lips had puffed up like someone had injected them full of air and her eyes had nearly swollen shut. You could practically see the hives spreading across her cheeks.

She must have seen the shocked looks on our faces because her hands reached for her own face. That's when she screamed.

"It's okay, Jones, just keep breathing," I said, trying to keep my voice as calm as possible. "I think she's having an allergic reaction to something. Is there anything in the lodge's first aid kit we might be able to give her?"

33

Amina stood there frozen.

"Amina, I think we need to give her something or get her to a hospital now," Joe insisted, snapping the assistant innkeeper out of her trance.

"Yes. Sorry. We keep a first aid kit behind the desk." Amina sprinted for the desk as I helped Jones into one of the lodge's wooden rocking chairs.

"Just try to stay calm. We're here to help," I reassured her.

"Little good you're doing," a nasally voice said as I felt someone elbow me out of the way. "The young woman is clearly having an anaphylactic reaction."

A dour-looking man in a fishing vest and waders pushed past me and leaned over Jones. "Are you having any trouble breathing?"

"N-no, I don't think so," she croaked. "My throat's a little swollen and I feel all tingly, but I can breathe okay."

"He nodded. "She doesn't seem to be going into shock, at least. Regardless, we're going to want to give her a shot of epinephrine. This could be a relatively minor episode or it could turn into something more severe. You don't want to take a chance with anaphylaxis. Thankfully, it's easily treatable as long as you know what you're doing. Not that anyone else at this establishment seems to know much of anything."

He looked around in annoyance for Amina. I could see Joe biting the inside of his cheek to keep from saying anything about the guy's attitude, and I was right there with him. But as much as I instantly disliked the guy, I was also grateful he'd shown up when he did. I'd had enough first aid training to know that anaphylaxis is a severe allergic reaction that requires urgent medical attention, and that epinephrine—which was another word for adrenaline—could reverse it. I'd never seen it happen to anyone before, though.

"Are you allergic to anything you know of?" I asked Jones.

Jones shook her head. "Maybe I'm just dehydrated?"

She raised the glass of iced tea to her mouth with a shaky hand.

"No!" Joe and I said at the same time. I grabbed the glass from her hand before it could reach her lips.

"Just in case something in the tea caused it," I said, setting the glass down beside me.

Amina stopped in the doorway with a large red first aid kit in her hands. "Our tea?!"

"Maybe not, but she could be allergic to one of the ingredients you used. Best to be safe until we know what caused the reaction," I told her.

"Give me that," the man snapped, grabbing the first aid kit from Amina. He rifled through the contents and pulled out a yellow plastic cylinder with the words EPINEPHRINE AUTO-INJECTOR on it. "Thank heavens this place managed to get something right."

"What is that?" Jones asked nervously.

"An EpiPen. It will deliver a shot of adrenaline that should treat the symptoms right away. Now hold out your leg."

Jones did. She only winced a little as the man pressed the

tube to her thigh muscle over her jeans and pushed down until it made a small click. He held it there for about ten seconds, then tossed it aside.

"They make these devices simple enough for a small child to use. You'd be advised to carry one around with you from now on in case this happens again."

The adrenaline went to work almost instantly.

"I—I think I'm okay," Jones said after a minute. She looked a little shell-shocked, and she still had hives and swelling, but that was a thousand times better than she'd looked before the shot. "Thank you for your help, Mr.—?"

"Doctor," he corrected snootily.

"Wow, it's a lucky break we had a physician nearby—" Jones began.

"Humph, not that kind of doctor," he said in a way that sounded like being a medical doctor was beneath him. "I have PhDs in multiple fields of biological research. You're just lucky my ex had a severe peanut allergy and had to carry an EpiPen with her everywhere we went."

"You're a scientist?" I asked. From his combination of profession and attitude, I had a good hunch who we were dealing with. "Do you know Max Kroopnik?"

The man's eyes narrowed. "Unfortunately. They'll let pretty much anybody pretend to be an expert on behavioral ecology these days." He dusted himself off like just being near us had made him dirty. "I've wasted enough time here. I have fishing to do."

He looked down at Jones before strutting off. "You're still going to want to visit the hospital. Sometimes a second reaction can occur, and I might not be around to save you."

There was a symphony of tooth grinding as Jones, Joe, and I all clenched our jaws and stared daggers at his back.

"Wow, Drawes is every bit as unpleasant as I thought he would be," Joe commented as the man we presumed to be Dr. Kroopnik's rival disappeared from sight.

Amina looked at Joe in surprise. "You already knew Dr. Drawes?"

"We knew *of* him," I said. I didn't want to say too much about our investigation in front of Amina, but Drawes hadn't done anything to help remove himself from our suspect list. "His cheery reputation precedes him."

Amina snorted. "He pays for a pass to go fishing on the grounds and likes to hang out in the lodge and treat everyone like his personal servants."

"Has he said anything about Dr. Kroopnik or his mountain lion research?" Joe asked.

"Not to me. Mostly he just orders me around and tells me how bad of a job I'm doing. We all do our best to steer clear of him."

Amina didn't seem to have much to add about Drawes besides another poor character reference. Further investigation was going to have to wait anyway. Suspect or not, Drawes's advice about Jones's allergy attack had been sound. "We'd better get Jones to the hospital just to be safe."

"Blerg," Jones groaned.

"The closest hospital is over an hour away," Amina said. "Dr. Feigelson in town is on call in case we ever have an emergency. She can be here in half the time. I think Jones will be more comfortable waiting for the doc here in one of our cozy beds than an emergency room."

Jones smiled. "That would be great, Amina, thanks."

"In the meantime," the assistant innkeeper added, addressing me and Joe, "you two can stow your gear at the back entrance of the lodge. Dan, our wilderness guide, is getting ready to take you to Black Bear, and he'll meet you in the back field with our all-terrain vehicles."

"You all did the right thing injecting her with epinephrine," Dr. Feigelson said a half hour later. I liked her right away. She was short with dark hair and a calm, laid-back vibe that put everyone in Jones's room at ease as soon as she entered. "That anaphylaxis could have been a lot worse if you hadn't acted so quickly. This kind of reaction isn't unheard-of in someone your age without any prior history of allergies, but it is less common. It would be helpful to know what caused it so you can take precautions to prevent it from happening again."

Jones shrugged. "Your guess is as good as mine. I've eaten all kinds of food and been bitten by all kinds of bugs, and nothing like this has ever happened."

"Well, you'll want to avoid the sun tea while you're here

just in case one of the ingredients triggered it, and I'd recommend scheduling an appointment with an allergist to run some tests when you get home. In the meantime, your body seems to be recovering well and you should be okay."

Jones sighed with relief and smiled in my direction. "That's great news. Black Bear Mountain isn't going to hike itself, and I've already put us behind schedule."

"Not so fast, young lady," Dr. Feigelson cautioned. "I said you're recovering well; I didn't say you're recovered. When you have an allergic reaction like that, there's still the chance of a second, biphasic reaction. It's not likely, but it does happen. It's also possible it was a plant or something else in the environment outside that caused your reaction. I need you in bed resting, where we can keep an eye on you, not trekking up the region's tallest, most remote mountain."

"But—" Jones started to protest.

"Doctor's orders. I'm sorry." Dr. Feigelson put a sympathetic hand on Jones's arm as she stood up. "I'll be back to check on you this evening."

Jones looked crestfallen.

"I'm going to stay here with you," I said.

Now Joe was the one who looked upset. "Dude! We still have a mission to go on! You know I'd never leave Jones behind if she was in real danger, but Dr. Feigelson said she should be okay. Max may not."

Jones placed her hand on the back of mine. "Joe is right, Frank. I'd feel a whole lot worse if you couldn't go because of me. I'm going to be fine. Dr. Kroopnik's your friend too, and right now he may need you a lot more than I do. Plus, I'll see what else I can find out about this treasure."

"We'll take good care of her," Amina said, turning to Jones. "The staff is going to pamper you like you're royalty."

I forced a smile. "Okay, Your Majesty. We'll see you in a couple days."

She gave me a playful shove. "Get out of here, you goofball, and go find your friend."

Leaving Jones behind to recover alone felt awful. So did my disappointment at not getting to spend more time with her. But she and Joe were right. Helping a friend who might be in danger had to come first.

"I'm going to give the rest of the lodge's crew instructions to make sure Jones gets anything she needs," Amina told us as we left Jones's room. "You guys can head out back. Your gear is already out there. Our wilderness guide, Dan, should have the ATVs ready to go for your ride out to Black Bear."

"Thanks for everything, Amina," I said as she hurried away.

"Have fun and stay safe," she called back over her shoulder. "I hope your scientist friend is okay."

Last time we'd been here, Commander Gonzo's Cessna had been waiting for us in the field behind the lodge. This time there were three four-wheel all-terrain vehicles. A tall, fit guy in his early twenties with short dark hair stood beside them.

"I wish Gonzo were around to fly us up there again," Joe said as we exited the lodge and walked toward the ATVs. "I was hoping to talk to both him and Dr. K about the helicopter flight simulation game I've been playing. It's not every day you get to talk flying with real pilots."

Thankfully, I'd had only one terrifying flight on our last trip. Joe had a second in the small chopper Dr. Kroopnik kept to fly in supplies to the mountaintop. My brother returned to Bayport obsessed with learning how to fly one himself. Our dad nixed the idea pretty quickly, so Joe spent hours on the computer practicing with a flight simulator instead.

"No offense, but I'm perfectly happy staying on the ground this time," I told him as we approached the guy with the ATVs.

"You must be Frank and Joe," he said, holding out his hand. "I'm Dan. I'll be leading you out to Black Bear Mountain."

"Sounds good to me," I said, giving his hand a shake. "I'm Frank."

"I've got your packs strapped onto my ride, so you guys don't have to worry about them," Dan said, shaking Joe's hand next. "The trails are going to get pretty bumpy and a lot muddy, so you may want to slide these on over your clothes so you don't end up a sopping mess."

He handed us each a jumpsuit to match his.

Joe inspected one of the ATVs and gave an impressed whistle. "Nice rides, dude. I'm still bummed we don't get to fly with Commander Gonzo, but these four-wheelers are a sweet alternative."

"We sure like them," Dan replied. "Brand-new, too."

"They're gas-electric hybrids!" I said, eyeing the green HYBRID emblems. I was nearly as excited as Joe. It was great to see the Bear Foot Lodge doing their part to help protect such a pristine woodland.

Dan grinned. "They sure are. ATVs are a great way to get around in the backcountry, but the air and noise pollution many of them cause can be a big problem in wilderness areas. Seems kinda backward, you know? Polluting the place you're enjoying while you ride them. But the emissions on these are super low, and they're way quieter."

"I heard these things were pretty pricey. Business must really be booming," Joe observed as he pulled on his suit.

"Oh, yeah, the last few seasons have been amazing. We've had all kinds of outdoors folks lining up to go on wilderness adventures. It's given me a chance to take guests all over the mountain range."

"Do you lead a lot of trips up to Black Bear Mountain?" I asked, zipping up my suit.

"Used to be not many people went up there. Now it's at the top of a lot of hikers' lists," Dan said.

"We heard it's not just hikers, either," Joe replied.

Dan gave him a confused look.

"What about hunters?" Joe prompted. "The kind who go looking for gems instead of animals?"

"Oh, um, yeah, I guess. Most of them are just amateur weekend warriors looking for a little excitement. No one ever finds anything, though," Dan shared. "I don't like taking them because they're usually less respectful of nature and try to go stomping all over the place. Half of them don't know a tent peg from a topographical map, and it's dangerous, too."

Joe and I knew that for a fact. Black Bear Mountain had nearly done us in a few times, and we were experienced outdoorsmen.

"They pay well, though." Dan shrugged.

"What about the one Amina said just got back?" I asked.

"Oh, the big fella with the buzz cut?" Dan asked. "That guy wasn't like the others. Came with his own ATV and all the right gear. You could tell he knew his way around the woods. Real in shape too. Decked out all in camo with a fighter-jet sticker on his truck, like he might have been in the military or something."

"How'd the hunt go? Did he find anything?" Joe asked casually.

"Don't know. I didn't take him. He booked a room and used us as base camp, but he knew exactly where he was going and didn't want a guide. Not real chatty, either. Just kept to himself. I asked him if he found anything when he got back, and he said to mind my own business."

"Did you get a name?" I prompted.

"He told the desk John Smith, but he was weird. We

usually keep a credit card on file for all our guests, but he said he didn't have one and paid in cash."

I didn't have to look at Joe to know we were thinking the same thing. A secretive guy with a military bearing and a generic name like John Smith who paid cash probably wasn't really named John Smith. It sounded like an alias, and people who use fake names usually have something to hide. I made a mental note of it. If Dr. K wasn't safe and sound in his research station, we'd be looking into it more.

"We'd better get a move on," I said, grabbing the helmet from the handlebar of my ATV and slipping it on. "We won't reach the research station before dark if we don't make up some time."

Dan gave a nervous look back at the lodge. "Yeah, um, I actually have some bad news for you guys. We're kind of shorthanded with Casey and Steven gone. I was booked this afternoon by a paying guest, so I'm only gonna be able to take you to the foot trail at the base of the mountain before heading back."

"So you're not guiding us all the way?" I asked. How many more surprises was this expedition going to have? We hadn't even left the lodge yet, and the only way it had gone was sideways.

Joe and I had extensive wilderness survival training, we'd mapped the seven-hour hike-and-climb ahead of time, and we'd come prepared with all the gear we thought we might need—after last time, we weren't taking any chances. But the "trails" on Black Bear Mountain were a lot closer to natural game trails than the neatly kept, easy-to-follow "nature trails" most hikers are used to. The terrain was as rugged as it gets and easy to get lost in. Or hurt. Sure, we were prepared, but it was the kind of trek you didn't want to do for the first time on your own if you could help it.

"Yeah, sorry about that," he said guiltily. "I'll get you where you need to go on the ATVs, but I've gotta bail on the hike up the maintain. If you guys want to cancel and not go at all, I'll understand."

The way he said it, it sounded like he was hoping that was what we'd do.

"Oh, no, we're going," Joe said right away. "With you or without you."

"We're prepared," I said confidently. At least that's how I hoped it sounded. It had taken all our skill and a good bit of luck to survive our last trip to Black Bear Mountain.

"Sure, sure, okay," Dan said defensively. "Casey said you're experienced hikers, and you've been up to Black Bear before, so you know the basic lay of the land, right? We bushwhacked and marked a new trail, so as long as you stick to that, you won't get lost. I've got pitons and rope ladders in place on the short verticals you have to scale, but Casey said you've done some climbing, too, so that shouldn't be a prob. You can radio from the old ranger station when you get there to check in and coordinate when you want me to come back to get you."

"Let's do this," Joe said, starting up his four-wheeler.

"You need a quick how-to on the ATVs before we get going?" Dan asked, slipping on his helmet.

Joe snapped his visor closed. "This isn't the first time we've gone off-road."

"Then follow me," Dan said, starting his up and accelerating across the field.

We followed Dan's lead along the river for a couple of miles before cutting off onto an off-road trail through the forest. The trail was a great new addition that hadn't been there on our first trip up to Black Bear Mountain. As concerned as I was about what we were leaving—Jones recovering in bed—*and* where we were going—Dr. K possibly missing on the mountain—watching the woods zip by from my ATV was exhilarating enough for me to lose myself in the moment.

Joe whooped it up in front of me as he caught air and splashed down in the creek ahead of us. The hybrids were way quieter than the gas version, especially when you were going slowly, but they were still loud enough that you had to yell to be heard when you were booking it like we were. I had to admit that I still felt a little guilty about disturbing the wildlife, but with Gonzo out of town, this was our only way to our destination. It was also a whole lot of fun.

"Whoo-hoo!" I hollered as my ATV sailed through the air into the creek.

The next hour passed in a blur of thrilling off-roading

and breathtaking scenery. For a bumpy off-road ride, it couldn't have gone more smoothly. Dan seemed nervous, though, and turned his head to look behind him every few minutes.

We emerged from the woods onto a path running alongside a large clearing leading to the foot of the mountain. In a few minutes we'd be there.

Telltale gnaw marks near the base of some of the trees clued me in that there was a beaver pond nearby. The stumps the beavers leave behind when they chew down trees to build their dams look a bit like spiked poles jutting out of the ground, and it was pretty cool to see their handiwork.

We reached the pond a minute later. Dan zipped past it with Joe not far behind.

I saw the shadow sweeping down over the trail before I saw the tree. The groan of the trunk snapping was loud enough that I could hear it over the engines. It took my brain a split second to compute what was happening. A split second may seem fast, but it wasn't fast enough to save my brother from riding straight into the path of the falling tree.

"Joe! Watch out!" I screamed as the large oak plummeted toward him.

TIMBER! 5

FRANK'S SCREAM REACHED ME AN INSTANT before the tree did. A few feet more and my ATV would be directly under it as it came crashing down. My first impulse was to hit the brakes, but as fast as the ATV was moving, stopping in time wasn't an option. The only thing left to do was speed up. I accelerated as much as I could. And then I closed my eyes.

The impact sounded like a cannon shot and set the ground shaking behind me. Which meant that I was still alive!

I opened my eyes, hit the brakes, and swung my ATV around to see Frank skid his to a stop just in time to keep from crashing into the oak now blocking his path. We

48

both whipped off our helmets and said at the same time, "Are you okay?!"

We nodded at each other from either side of the fallen tree.

"Whoa, are you guys both all right?" Dan yelled, racing back toward us and pulling to a stop.

"Well, I think we solved one mystery," I said. "If a tree falls in the woods and someone is there to almost be crushed by it, it definitely makes a sound."

"I'd laugh if my heart weren't pounding so fast," said Frank, climbing off his ATV. "I thought it was going to crush you, for sure."

"You nearly crashed into it too," I reminded him. "It could have flattened us both."

"I've spent a lot of time in the woods, but that's the wildest random act of nature I've ever seen." Dan walked over to look at the split base of the tree, where it looked like a beaver had chewed either end nearly into spikes. "The beavers must've left just enough wood there to keep it standing when they stopped. I guess us zooming by like that was all the shaking it needed to tumble over."

"That's what it looks like on the surface," Frank said, reaching down and yanking at something by his feet. "Under the surface, there's a trip wire."

"A what?!" Dan gawked.

I examined the nearly pointy stump left sticking out of the ground. When I looked closely, teeth marks weren't the only marks I saw.

"The beavers chewed only part of the way. Someone used an ax to do the rest."

Dan looked back and forth between Frank and me. "I—I don't understand."

Frank gave the tripwire a twang. "Either you have some super-industrious beavers, or this is sabotage."

"Sabotage?!" Dan gasped. "But why?"

"Either someone has a really sick idea of a practical joke—" Frank began.

"Or someone knew we were coming and laid a trap to take us out," I finished.

"Looks like they set it up expecting multiple vehicles, so when the first one came through, it would catch the wire and the force would pull the tree the rest of the way down to fall in the path of the other riders," said Frank.

"But who would do something like that?" Dan wondered nervously.

"Someone who knew we were on our way to Black Bear Mountain to check on Dr. Kroopnik and didn't want us to find him," I speculated.

"This is out of control. You can't go up there by yourselves," Dan insisted.

"We wouldn't have to if you hadn't bailed on us," I said.

"No way I'd go up there with you now, even if I didn't have to get back," he said. "Bears and mountain lions, I'm cool with. People who set traps to take me out, no thank you. You two aren't thinking straight if you don't hop on those ATVs and follow me back to the lodge. You won't even have cell phone service to call for help if anything else happens."

The look of determination on Frank's face said it all. Any doubts I'd had about Aleksei's fears that Dr. K was in danger vanished with Frank's discovery of that trip wire. We'd set out to make sure our friend was safe, and that was exactly what we were going to do.

"Not a chance," I said.

Dan shook his head like we were delusional as he unstrapped our packs from the back of his ATV. "The lodge isn't going to be liable if you go up there and some killer comes after you."

"We'll take our chances," said Frank.

"Suit yourselves." Dan gunned his ATV around the fallen tree and headed back the way we'd come.

"Well, that's not how I envisioned this expedition starting," Frank said as we watched him vanish into the distance. He pulled a pad and pen from his pack and pinned it to the fallen tree. "To let any other hikers who come along know the ATV trail may not be safe."

Using the smaller, less used paths, we rode slowly the long way around the beaver pond to avoid any other possible traps and stayed off the main path until we reached the foot trail at the base of the mountain. We stowed the ATVs in the brush beside the trail, grabbed our packs, and stepped into the woods.

"With all these setbacks, I don't think we're going to make Dr. K's research station before the sun starts to set." Frank sighed. "Is it just me, or did you think Dan was acting squirrelly even before that tree fell?"

"He sure seemed nervous about something, especially the way he kept looking behind him on the way here," I agreed. "Do you think *he* could have been in on the trap?"

"Riding past that tree would have been a pretty big risk to take, but he was the first one to go, and it was rigged to fall on whoever was behind him," Frank said.

"He seemed as shocked by it as we were, though," I countered.

"Doesn't mean he wasn't acting," said Frank.

I took a second to consider it. "He did seem pretty intent on us not coming up here."

"To be fair, this expedition does seem a little reckless," Frank said. "You know, seeing as someone is trying to drop trees on us and all."

"Whoever it is might still be lying in wait somewhere along the trail, so let's stay sharp," I warned.

Like Dan had said, there were trail markers tacked to the trees along the path. The terrain was steep, rugged, and slow going, but I love a good wilderness challenge, and I would have been stoked about every second of it under normal circumstances. Our circumstances definitely weren't normal, though. Not with Dr. K missing and the possibility of treasure hunters trying to kill us. A hike this difficult requires close attention to every step—especially when it might be booby-trapped—and it didn't help that we also had to stay on high alert for potential perps lurking in the woods.

Rays of sun poked through the dense canopy of trees, splattering the forest floor with blotches of light. The direction of the beams and quality of the light changed as the day went on until the light started to turn golden.

"It's closing in on sunset and we still have a few more hours of hiking to go," Frank said, peering up at the patches of sky visible through the canopy of the pine grove we were in.

I peered ahead at a steep ledge that was going to require some climbing. "That bad boy could be tricky, and we probably don't want to tackle it in fading light."

I took a look around the pine grove. The incline wasn't bad, and there was a little clearing off to the side where we could safely make a fire.

Frank was thinking the same thing. "Let's camp here for the night and get started again at first light. I don't like the idea of leaving Max out there alone any longer than we have to, but it won't do him any good if we get ourselves hurt or lost in the dark."

"Great minds, bro," I said, unzipping my bag. "I'm excited to try out our new hammocks. Stealth mode is going to come in extra handy if someone really is out there hunting us. Once we cook dinner and put out the fire, it will be like we vanished."

Instead of a conventional tent, we'd packed two tree tents, which were basically hammock-tent hybrids. If anybody—or any*thing*—came looking for us on the ground, we'd be safely tucked away above their heads, suspended between two trees all snuggly in our cocoons.

We wouldn't be the only thing suspended between two trees, either. So would our food. As soon as we were done eating, we wrapped everything up in a "bear" bag and hung it ten feet off the ground and well outside our camp. Black Bear Mountain didn't get its name by accident, and we'd learned last time how much trouble a hungry bear could cause if it wandered into camp. Black bears were rarely a threat to humans, but they had great sniffers and weren't above mooching a pack of hot dogs or flapjacks off unsuspecting campers.

There was one more precaution we took, and this one was more for predators of the human variety. We'd walked the perimeter of our campsite before the sun sent, and we'd both been keeping an ear out for any suspicious sounds in the woods. We couldn't be certain, but if anyone was out there spying on our camp, they'd hidden themselves well.

We stashed the rest of our gear on the ground nearby, camouflaged under some brush, doused the fire with water from a nearby brook, and climbed up into our hammocks. With all the danger we were facing, I expected to have trouble falling asleep, but we'd burned a lot of energy on the hike, and I was out cold the instant I closed my eyes.

When I opened them again, it was to the sound of Frank's snores. At least that's what I thought at first. Only these weren't coming from the tree next to me—they were coming from below. Then it hit me that I'd heard a similar sound on our last trip as well, and it wasn't snoring. It was grunting. And it was coming from a bear.

Okay, so it's more than a little unnerving to have a bear rummaging around right under you. Logically, though, I knew it wasn't really a threat, especially with us up in a tree without any food on us. I took a deep breath, silently gave thanks for our hammocks, and decided to leave the bear alone instead of trying to make a lot of noise and scare it off. Sure, that might work, but it would also call all kinds of attention to ourselves. If there was a *human* predator out there lurking in the woods, we might as well just start shouting, *Come and get us, bad guys!* Nope. Better just to let the bear rummage around and be on its merry bear way.

It was when I heard the sound of fabric tearing that I realized what it was rummaging through. The packs with all our gear!

6

HONEY BEAR

FRANK

"GET AWAY, BEAR! GET!" ARE NOT THE words you want to wake up to while camping.

I probably would have tumbled right out of my hammock if the tent flap hadn't been zipped. It took me a confused minute to get the zipper undone and poke my head out. When I did, I saw Joe's flashlight beam focused on the ample rear end of a large black bear as it lumbered out of the pine grove, carrying something in its mouth.

"Wait! Get back here, bear! That's ours! We need that!" Joe yelled.

"Uh-oh," I muttered as I shone my own flashlight down at bits and pieces of chewed-up gear scattered on the forest floor. "That was the pack with all our survival gear, wasn't it?"

"Including my Swiss Army knife," Joe groaned, climbing out of his hammock and down the tree to inspect the aftermath of the bear's raid. "I don't get it. We made sure there wasn't any food left in those bags at all."

I climbed down after him, carefully shining my light around the grove to make sure we were alone.

"At least he only ran off with one of the packs," Joe said, holding up a torn but otherwise intact backpack. "Too bad the one he left is the nearly empty one where we kept the hammocks and the bear bag with the food. The maps, GPS, water purification filters, and the rest of the stuff we brought to help us stay alive out here is gone."

"That doesn't make any sense. We were careful to wrap all our food up tightly before packing it, but if either bag had residual food scent on it, it would be that one."

I moved my light over the stuff that had fallen out of the pack the bear ran off with. A torn rain poncho. A pair of thermal socks newly in need of darning. A pocket-size guide to identifying edible plants. And—

"Our GPS!" I ran over to pick up the handheld device. If there was anything we might really need to help us get off the mountain in a pinch, that was it. Or, it would have been if the screen wasn't a spiderweb of cracked glass and bear-tooth puncture holes. Oddly, that wasn't the most unusual thing about it.

"What the—" I mumbled to myself as I peeled my fingers from the back of the broken device. There was something golden and sticky smeared all over it. I smelled the gooey residue the GPS left on my fingers. I didn't know what bear slobber smelled like, but I was pretty sure it wasn't nearly this appetizing.

I turned to Joe. "I know what lured the bear to our packs. Honey."

"But we didn't bring any honey," he said, confused.

"That's why I said 'lured,'" I replied. "I don't think that bear raiding our gear was any more an accident than the tree falling in our path at the beaver pond. Black bears have some of the most sensitive noses in the wild kingdom, and they love the smell of honey. I bet a lot of other wild animals do too. I packed the GPS at the bottom of the bag, and there's only one easy way to explain how bear bait got all over the gear at the bottom of our pack."

"Someone put it there to bait critters in an attempt to waylay us on our way up the mountain." Joe swept his flashlight back around the pine grove. If there was a bad guy hiding behind a tree, we didn't see him.

"So far whoever it is has tried to sabotage us from a distance," I said. "They haven't attacked us directly."

"Yet," Joe said, giving the area another sweep with his light.

"Who is the common denominator in both attempts?" I asked. It didn't take Joe long to get where I was going.

"Dan loaded the ATVs and was alone with our gear for at least a half hour while we were looking after Jones," he said. "Amina wasn't with the us the whole time either. She seemed nice, but we don't really know her."

Amina's name got me thinking in a different direction. This one was just as ominous, and Joe and I weren't the victims. "Amina also had access to something else besides honey. What if Jones's allergy attack wasn't an accident after all?"

Joe seemed to consider it.

"Amina knew we were coming and why, and she would have had the opportunity to spike the tea," I added.

Joe raised a skeptical eyebrow. "Seems like a stretch. How would she know Jones had an allergy when Jones herself didn't even know? We also can't be sure it was the tea that did it and not something else."

"You're probably right. Everything looks suspicious at the moment, but sometimes an accident is just an accident," I conceded. "But whoever it is, we have to consider the possibility that beavers and bears aren't their only accomplices. We don't know what we're going to find at the top of the mountain or how Dr. K plays into this yet, but we could be facing multiple perps."

"We know Drawes is out there somewhere and has a motive to cause Dr. K harm," Joe said. "John Smith is another wild card. We know he's after the garnets, which gives him a motive as well, whoever he is."

"There's one other ex–treasure hunter we do know the name of," I said as I worked through the theory in my mind. "He has an alibi, but—"

"It wouldn't be the first time Steven conspired to steal Aleksei's demantoids," Joe completed the thought for me.

"He and Casey both being away while we're here does seem pretty convenient."

"Casey told me on the phone that she had to go to a hospitality conference, which seems pretty legit, but we don't if Steven is with her," I said. "With the lodge doing as well as it is, you'd think one of the owners would want to stay behind so they aren't so shorthanded."

"It's hard to imagine Casey doing anything like this, not after seeing how devastated she was last time when she found out what Steven and her sister had done," I said. "And as badly as things went for Steven that time, would he really have the guts to try again?"

"Speaking of people we know have guts . . . ," Joe started, but he cut himself short. From the pained look on his face, I could tell something was bothering him.

"Joe, what is it?"

"You're not going to like this, Frank, but the person with the easiest access to our gear from the moment we arrived is Jones."

"No way," I snapped. "I know you feel threatened by me including Jones in our investigations, but to call her a suspect is ridiculous."

"Dude, I am so not threatened by Jones—okay, maybe a little," he admitted. "But that's not what this is about. I think Jones is awesome, and she's totally carried her weight as a detective. The idea that she might be involved upsets me, too. I'm just saying it's *possible*."

"It's not possible," I shot back.

"Just hear me out, okay?" he asked. "I'm not saying she did it, but she did have the means and the opportunity. She had prior knowledge of the original case from when you were going out and knew about our hunch that Aleksei had a secret stash of garnets. She's also the one who had the idea to come along on this trip as soon as you told her where we were going."

"I can't believe this. Are you really suggesting *Jones* would try double-cross us and find the gems for herself?" I laughed. "And, what, you think she also conspired to have a potentially deadly allergy attack?"

"It's not the most outrageous thing to ever happen on one of our cases," he said. "I didn't think about it until you mentioned the possibility of Amina spiking her tea. I don't think Amina could have because she wouldn't have a way of knowing Jones had a secret allergy. The only person who could know is Jones." He saw me about to rebut him and interjected before I could. "I know, I know, poisoning yourself with an allergen to misdirect suspicions would be an extreme measure, but it sure would create an impressive alibi."

"Are you sure that tree didn't actually fall on your head?" I asked him. "You're going to have better luck convincing me the bear that stole our pack is a criminal mastermind. Jones isn't involved in any way. End of story."

Joe held up his hands in defeat. "Sorry, bro. Just trying to explore every angle, that's all."

"Well, that one's a dead end," I said, putting the conversation to rest. I admit my feelings for Jones made me a little biased. Objectivity is critical to any good investigation, and objectively Joe was right about Jones having the means and opportunity—and we both knew from experience that really good people were sometimes capable of doing bad things. But I also knew from experience that intuition is one of the best tools a good detective has, and my intuition told me that Jones was a true friend and would *never* do something like that.

I looked up at the lightening dawn sky. "So much for a full night's rest. Let's take stock of the gear we have left and get moving. The sun should be up for us to climb that ledge soon."

"Well, we have all our food at least, so we won't starve, and a pot to boil stream water in if we run out of H2O," he said, holding up the metal water bottle he'd kept with him in his hammock.

We also had the pocket survival kits we always carried, my Swiss Army knife, a hatchet, and the new paracord bracelet Cherry from the general store had given Joe.

Joe held up his wrist and tapped the little compass that was woven into it. "The original mountain men didn't need GPS, and neither do we. It would be nice to have a map, but in a pinch, we can always get our bearings. And right now, our bearing is north!"

The rest of the trek up the mountain was tense but thankfully uneventful. We were both on high alert for danger, but the most ominous things we faced were an angry squirrel and some mosquitoes. Two hours later we were crouched in the brush, staring up at the old ranger station lookout that doubled as Dr. K's research station and residence.

The old ranger cabin sat perched atop one-story-tall wooden stilts at the edge of a ravine, overlooking a gnarly set of river rapids rushing down the mountainside below. The cabin had windows all the way around to give rangers a 360-degree view over the entire mountain range, so they could spot any forest fires for miles. The station was surrounded by a gated wooden fence with bold NO TRESPASSING signs—neither of which had been there last time.

There was another change too. A new wooden rope bridge was suspended over the rapids, leading from the cabin's wraparound deck to the other side of the ravine.

Joe shuddered when he saw it. The bridge was new because the last one had torn apart when Joe was tossed over the side during our last trip. That was right after I'd found Max tied up and gagged in his own specimen cabinet. And that was right before I'd plunged over a waterfall in a tiny raft. Max had gone over the falls with me, and the wipeout had left him with a permanent limp.

"Let's hope this visit goes better than the last one," said Joe.

I immediately realized something wasn't right this time either.

"The door is open," I whispered. "I don't think Dr. K would have left it that way, not with all the expensive equipment and delicate specimens he keeps in there."

Joe jumped up to run to the station. I grabbed his arm and held him back.

"Let's lie low and conduct surveillance for a while before we head to the station, in case anyone is hiding up there," I said. "If nothing moves, then we move in."

One of the hardest parts of being a detective is having patience, especially when a friend may be in danger. Rushing in and potentially getting ourselves into a jam right along with Max wouldn't have done any of us any good. So we watched and waited. When nothing moved for a half hour, we did. We approached cautiously, with Joe leading the way and me lingering a few yards behind in case anyone sprang an ambush and he needed backup.

The smell hit me right away.

"Skunk," I whispered.

It got stronger the closer we got.

"Really skunky skunk," Joe whispered as we approached.

We reached the base of the stilts safely, but it was on the climb up that we were most vulnerable. We'd be an open target for anyone hiding on the ground, and anyone lying in wait inside had the upper ground, so we moved up the steps as quickly as we could without compromising safety.

The skunk smell got even skunkier when we reached the deck, skunky enough to make our eyes water.

I lifted my head and peeked quickly into the window of the back room. I gave Joe the *okay* hand sign to indicate it was all clear. Then I crawled toward the main room on my hands and knees, careful to stay out of view of the windows. I raised my head and gave another peek.

I could tell two things right away: (1) there wasn't anybody in the main room, which took up most of the station, and (2) someone other than Dr. K had been there recently—and they'd torn the place apart.

There was scientific equipment knocked over and scattered everywhere. My heart hurt for all Dr. K's research. My only hope was that the scientist was in better shape than his field lab.

"The main area looks clear," I whispered.

"I'm going in," Joe said, peering through the open door and nodding back at me before standing up and stepping inside. I quickly followed him.

His eyes locked on the empty surface where Dr. K usually kept the shortwave radio that allowed him to communicate with the outside world. All that was left were a few shredded cords. "The radio is gone. No wonder no one's been able to reach him."

"From the look of those cupboards, the only things to have eaten a meal here in a while are the wildlife," I said, observing the empty, shredded food containers littering the counter and floor. "Based on the mold growth on that banana peel, I'd say it's been a few days at least, maybe longer."

"Are those animal turds?" Joe cringed as he eyed the little mounds scattered on the floor.

We both froze at the sound of something moving behind

a knocked-over specimen cabinet. I gulped back panic as the intruder stepped into sight. I had been wrong about the station being unoccupied, and the current inhabitant definitely wasn't Max Kroopnik. The intruder had beady eyes and dark black hair with a fat white streak running down the center. We were standing face-to-face with a skunk.

EVERYTHING SMELLS LIKE FLOWERS

7

JOE

I DON'T THINK I'VE EVER BEEN SO AFRAID OF something so cute. I've faced down a lot of bad guys and girls before, and some of them even smelled like they could have used a shower. None of them made my knees quake the way that skunk did.

The sulfury odor filling Dr. K's ransacked research station was potent enough to make my eyes tear up, and I had a feeling the skunk's funk wasn't even that recent—whatever it had sprayed was long gone by the time we got there. I didn't want to find out what it smelled like freshly sprayed all over me.

The skunk looked around blindly like it knew we were there but couldn't see us, even though it was a few feet away. From the way it was wiggling its pointy black nose and sniffing at the air, it could smell us, though. And we could *definitely* smell it.

Frank put his finger to his lips, signaling me to be quiet, and slowly started backing out the door. I followed his lead, resisting the urge to turn and run screaming instead. About halfway down the stairs, I breathed a sigh of relief. The skunk hadn't followed us. It looked like we were out of the blast zone and in the clear.

"Talk about a contaminated crime scene," I said.

"Looks like it's going to stay that way too," Frank replied. "I don't think we're going to be doing much up-close investigating while that skunk is using Max's place as a vacation rental."

"I can imagine the online reviews now," I said.

"Skunks are usually nocturnal, so I'm guessing we woke it up from its beauty sleep," said Frank, slipping into junior naturalist mode again. "They have bad eyesight, but their sense of smell and hearing are great. I was afraid if we made any more noise, it might feel threatened and spray us. Thankfully, they usually only use their scent as a last resort."

"From the smell up there, that skunk last-resorted someone recently," I said as we reached terra firma.

"I hope it was the perp and not Max that got hit," Frank said. "That smell can last up to two weeks or longer if you don't have a special solution to remove it with."

"At least we'll smell them coming," I said, giving myself a sniff as well to make sure I hadn't accidentally picked up a free sample of Eau de Skunk cologne.

"What I want to know is why there's a critter living in Dr. K's outpost instead of Dr. K," Frank said, staring back up at the station with concern.

"That skunk isn't the only thing about this situation that stinks, that's for sure." I scanned the woods around the tower. "Let's head for cover in case the burglar comes back. Whoever it is doesn't mind using violence, and there are things worse than skunk spray we could be shot with."

"It definitely wasn't just four-legged animals that tore that place apart," Frank noted as he followed me. "Someone was looking for something, and you can bet it's the garnets."

"I'm just hoping them taking the radio means they're trying to hide it from Dr. K so he can't call for help," I said. "At least that way we'd know he was okay."

"Or at least he was," Frank replied ominously. "We don't know what's happened since then."

I snapped my fingers—my brain must have wanted me to look on the bright side, because a mental lightbulb had just flicked on. "The missing radio reminds me of something. It's not the only one Dr. K had access to."

"The chopper!" Frank exclaimed.

I took off running, with Frank right behind.

"There it is," I whispered, peering over a small hill not far from the ranger station.

"If the chopper's still here, then we know Max didn't just fly away and leave the mountain," Frank whispered back. "He's got to still be out here in the wilderness somewhere."

We approached the chopper slowly, carefully looking around to make sure we were still alone. We were going to have to take every step like there was someone in the woods hunting us—because there probably was.

And it looked like whoever it was had already beaten us to Dr. K's chopper. The radio had been smashed.

Groan. "Which means we can't call for help, either."

The radio wasn't the only thing in pieces. The control panel had been pulled apart.

"There's a reason Dr. K didn't just fly away. He couldn't."

"So where do we go from here?" Frank asked as we moved off into the brush to get back out of sight. Always the nature nerd at heart, I could see him taking mental note of a showy shrub with little star-shaped yellow flowers.

"Where would Dr. K go is the better question," I replied. I didn't add the other part that crossed my mind: *assuming he got away.*

"This is one of the non-native species from the Ural Mountains that Aleksei planted from seeds he brought with him. They don't grow in this part of the world normally," Frank noted absently before returning to the topic at hand. "We know Aleksei had a few hideouts on the mountain where he lived all those years. If Max knows someone is after him, he could be lying low in one of them."

"Only we have no way of knowing where they are. We also know he had secret hiding places for the demantoids, but we don't know how to find those either." I kicked at the dirt in frustration as we walked, sending pebbles skittering into another one of Aleksei's Ural Mountain shrubs with the yellow star-shaped flowers.

When I looked up, Frank was running over to another yellow-flowered shrub about twenty feet away. I recognized the junior botanist gleam in his eyes right away as he knelt down to examine it. Leave it to my brother to get all excited about a plant while we're imperiled on a remote mountaintop.

"Bro, you can fondle the flora later. We've kinda got an urgent mystery to solve, in case you hadn't noticed," I chastised him.

"Oh, that's not all I noticed," he said with a cocky grin. "I think Aleksei may have planted a clue to where his hideouts are."

"I feel like there's a bad pun in there, but I don't quite catch it," I said, wondering what Frank was up to. "I know those are one of the non-native flowers Aleksei brought with him from Siberia, but we already established that."

"We know he planted a bunch of the seeds to make the mountain feel more like home when he first got here, but what if they're not just decorative? What if . . ." Frank got up and dashed another few yards down the hill.

This time I ran after him. His destination? Another identical yellow-flowered shrub exactly twenty feet away.

"They're trail markers!" I said.

"We've passed patches around the mountain with a variety of different Ural Mountain plants where Aleksei cultivated little flower gardens in the woods. And there are other places where they've gone wild and are scattered around randomly—" Frank began, but by this time I knew exactly where he was going.

"Only these are spaced at precise intervals with only regular native plants growing around them in between."

"There's so much other vegetation around here that to an untrained eye, it just looks like normal mountain forest. Only someone who already knew what to look for would notice the pattern in the anomalous specimens." Frank grinned proudly. "That or an expertly attuned naturalist."

"My apologies for ever doubting you, bro," I said. "If I could give you an honorary doctorate in flower power, I would."

"Let's follow the Yellow Shrub Trail!" he said, marching ahead.

"Just please tell me Black Bear Mountain doesn't have evil flying monkeys, because skunks and bears are bad enough," I groaned. "Oh, and I refuse to skip."

The trail grew harder to follow as the brush grew thicker, and there were some other, smaller baby shrubs here and there, where seeds must have fallen naturally. Sure enough, though, there was a bigger one of the same size every twenty feet.

I didn't have to skip to follow the trail, but I did have to whack. The brush soon grew thick enough that the only option was to hack our way through with my hatchet.

"This job would be a lot easier with a machete," I griped.

We'd planned the trip knowing we might have to do some bushwhacking, and we'd packed a machete for just that purpose—only we packed it in the bag the bear ran off with.

"I really hate that bear right about now," Frank muttered as he disentangled himself from yet another thornbush.

Every so often we'd get a faint whiff of skunk. I couldn't tell if the smell was just stuck up my nostrils or what. I know it's not unusual for the woods—this was skunk home turf, after all—but it was still disconcerting after our recent Close Encounter of the Stinky Kind. Knowing our luck so far, there were probably skunks sleeping under every rock, just waiting for us to step on them so they could spray us.

Thankfully, if there were, we didn't see them. The other thing we didn't see was Aleksei's hideout. We hadn't seen much of anything except for trees and dense undergrowth.

"Talk about off the beaten path," I groaned, my socks squishing inside my boots from the overgrown marsh we'd just trudged through.

We were covered in dirt, sweat, and scratches, and I was just about to toss down my hatchet and take a nap under one of Aleksei's yellow-starred shrubs when we finally emerged from the brush.

"Finally, a change of scenery," Frank said, picking one of the little yellow flowers from the trail-marking shrub at the edge of the brush.

Twenty feet later we found ourselves on the edge of a

little ravine with a large fallen tree stretched across it like a bridge. What we didn't find was another yellow, star-flowered shrub.

"Either the Yellow Shrub Trail is a dead end—" I began.

"Or Aleksei has a hideout on the other side of that ravine," Frank finished optimistically. He pointed to a neat row of tall bushes. "See how those elder bushes are growing in a line? They wouldn't grow that way naturally. Someone had to plant them. I bet what we're looking for is on the other side!"

"Well, let's go find out," I said, stepping carefully onto the fallen tree. I'd had one tree almost fall on me today; I didn't want to fall *off* another one.

When we pushed through the bushes on the other side, there was a tiny, vine-covered cabin. It was well enough camouflaged that you'd never see it from a distance, and even if you stumbled right upon it, you might not notice it unless you were already looking.

"That's it!" Frank mouthed excitedly. We didn't know what we would find inside, and it was best not to announce our presence.

Brush had grown up around it like it hadn't been tended in a while. When we stepped closer, you could see where it had been recently stepped on and pushed aside by a large animal. *Or* a person. And from the way the disturbed brush led straight to the closed front door, I was betting on the latter. I tried peeking through one of the vine-covered windows, but the shutters were closed, blocking my view. We were going to have to go in blind.

I gently placed my hand on the door and looked at Frank, who nodded. Then I pushed, and the door opened with a groan.

And then . . . silence. The cabin was empty.

It was also itty-bitty. There was a stone fireplace against the back wall, a little built-in table on one side, a wooden sleeping loft barely large enough for someone Aleksei's size to squeeze into on the other side, and a couple of bare shelves.

"I know tiny houses are all the rage, but this kinda makes me question the trend, especially for a dude as big as Aleksei," I commented. Our burly friend had a big heart and an even bigger body. "This is barely bigger than a cubby for someone his size."

"Judging by all the dust and mouse droppings, I don't think anyone has used it for a long time," Frank said, squatting down to examine one of the boot prints in the dust. "Until the last few days, that is. These prints are fresh."

"Yeah," I agreed as I puzzled over the trail in the dust. "And they lead in one direction. Straight to the fireplace. Whoever entered never left."

I could feel the hairs on my arm rise from the weirdness of it.

"There aren't exactly a lot of places they could have gone," Frank observed, looking around the claustrophobic little space. "Not unless they climbed up the chimney."

"Either that, or this tiny house isn't as tiny as it seems," I said, thinking about one of Aleksei's other hobbies.

We both smiled as we pulled out our flashlights and knelt down by the fireplace to investigate the stone for anything that looked or felt out of place. I had to reach my arm as far up the chimney as it would go before I felt the chain.

I yanked. Stone creaked against stone as the fireplace floor rose.

We knew Aleksei was fond of traps and disguises. His tiny cabin in the woods contained both. The fireplace was really a trapdoor.

BIG THINGS, SMALL PACKAGES

8

FRANK

LOOKS LIKE ALEKSEI'S TINY HOUSE ISN'T so tiny after all," I said, shining my flashlight through the fireplace trapdoor into the enormous cavern below.

"Whoa, he must have built the cabin right on top of an entrance to a natural cave system." Joe stepped onto the rope ladder attached to the inside wall. "Here goes something."

"Be right down," I called, as Joe reached the bottom. First I wanted to close the cabin's front door so as not to tip off anyone who might be tracking us. A gust of breeze carried the smell of forest flowers into the cabin. That and skunk.

I shook off my sense of unease and followed Joe through the trapdoor. A second chain dangled next to the ladder. I gave it a tug and the trapdoor closed back up again. Aleksei sure made inventive use of all those decades of mountain seclusion.

The cavern was ten times the size of the cabin and three times as high, with an arched opening at one end that looked like it might lead to a side passage. There was a handmade bed at the other end of the cavern, along with jars of preserved and dried food and a few cracked glass jugs that might have once contained water. Partially burned candles had been set into little cubbies in the cavern walls.

"Looks like this was Aleksei's doomsday cave," Joe said. "And from the look of these boot tracks, he wasn't the only one to use it."

"Someone else has definitely been here very recently," I agreed, noting how the dirt had been swept aside near the bed as if someone had pushed it and then moved it back—which was exactly what I did next.

Hidden underneath was a square hole about four inches by four inches in size. Nestled inside was a little wooden chest.

"I think you'll want to see this," I called to Joe, who was exploring the opening on the other side of the cavern.

I waited until he was by my side to pull the box from the hole and lift the lid. I knew instantly from the rainbow twinkle of prismatic light that refracted back when Joe's flashlight hit it that this was where Aleksei's demantoid garnets had been. Why do I say *had been*? Because the only thing left was some sparkling green garnet dust at the bottom of the box.

"The gems are gone," Joe said. "And I think I know who took them."

He shined his light down at the boot prints leading away from the garnets' hiding spot. "I noticed a pattern in the boot tracks over by that opening."

The pattern jumped out at me now that I knew to look for it. "The right boot makes a distinct track, while the left boot leaves a slight drag mark behind it." I took a second to think about what it meant. "Whoever was here had a limp."

Joe nodded at me encouragingly. Then I had it. "Dr. K!" I declared. I walked toward the opening, trying to discern more clues from the boot prints.

"The tracks move around the cave like he was here for a while before leaving. We know from the one-way tracks in the cabin that he came in the front door but didn't exit," I deduced. I shined my light into the opening, illuminating the entrance to a naturally occurring subterranean tunnel that twisted out of the cavern into darkness. "This tunnel passage is the only other exit I see. Dr. K must have gone down here—wherever it leads."

"You don't think Dr. Kroopnik could have stolen the garnets for himself, do you?" Joe asked. "He's Aleksei's best friend."

"I—I don't know. This wouldn't be the first time someone staged their own disappearance on Black Bear Mountain in order to get away with a crime. It's straight out of Aleksei's playbook, actually. We're going to have to locate Max to find out." I turned my flashlight back toward the tunnel opening.

We were both stepping in that direction when the sound of the cabin door closing carried down to us from above. We froze and looked up at the trapdoor. What we heard next was the muted thud of footsteps on the cabin's plank floor. There was also a slight draft of breeze drifting down into the cavern from the fireplace. It carried with it the unmistakable odor of skunk.

"That sure doesn't sound like a skunk," Joe whispered nervously.

It suddenly hit me why the faint odor of skunk we kept smelling on the bushwhacking trek to the cabin had unsettled me so much. It wasn't skunk we were smelling. It was whoever had gotten sprayed by the skunk we'd run into in Dr. K's research station.

"That has to be the perp who ransacked Dr. K's lab," I whispered with a sinking feeling in my gut. "They must have been tracking us from a distance with binoculars the whole time. We led them right here."

Joe winced at our gaffe. "It's not going to take Stinky long to see the tracks going in but not out and reach the same conclusion we did about the trapdoor in the fireplace."

The footsteps stopped right at the fireplace. The next thing we heard was the cold metallic *CLICK-CLACK* of a gun being racked.

I gulped. My Swiss Army knife and Joe's hatchet weren't going to do us much good against a gun-wielding assailant.

"Time to make our exit," Joe said, echoing my thoughts.

"Hopefully the exit is down here," I said, making a beeline for the opening. "Because that's our only option."

Our footsteps echoed off the stone walls as we snaked our way through the narrow tunnel toward an unknown destination.

"I see light!" Joe called a few minutes later as the sound of the perp's footsteps began to echo into the underground lair from somewhere behind us.

Sure enough, there was an exit straight ahead. Vines cascaded over it from the outside like a natural curtain, disguising it from view. A handmade wooden grate that Aleksei must have used to keep animals out had been pushed aside.

"Freedom!" I exclaimed, my heart lightening as I parted the vines, allowing the fresh breeze to sweep away the stale cave air and sunlight to pierce the darkness, temporarily blinding me.

"Um, by freedom, did you mean the side of a sheer cliff with no way down?" Joe asked dubiously from behind me as I blinked the spots away from my eyes.

I instantly wished I hadn't, because I was looking straight down at a fifty-foot drop into a canyon filled with sharp rocks.

NOWHERE TO GO BUT DOWN

9

JOE

THE CAVE DR. K USED AS AN ESCAPE route didn't just lead to a dead end. It led to a dead drop. A torn bit of rope dangled from a rusty piton that had been driven into the lip of the cave. There had been a way down. Once. I had no way of knowing how long the rope had been, but it must have led to a place where someone could safely descend the cliff. Wherever that place was, we couldn't see it, let alone try to reach it.

"How did Max make it down without the rope?" I wondered aloud.

"I'm a little more concerned with how we're going to make it down," Frank fretted as the echo of Stinky's footsteps through the cave grew closer. We had a few minutes at most to devise an escape.

A flash of white fabric caught my eye in the trees on the other side of the canyon. I quickly unzipped our remaining backpack and pulled out my cell phone. The phone may have been useless without reception, but the camera still worked.

"You're taking pictures?!" Frank squeaked.

"Just getting a closer look," I said, zooming in as far as the camera would go. "The bear took our binoculars, so I'm improvising."

The white object grew larger as I zoomed. At first I thought it was a white sheet tangled up in the limbs, but as I got closer, the cords dangling from the edges came into view. "I think I know how Max got down. He jumped."

"He what?!"

"With a parachute."

"He didn't leave two others lying around, did he?" Frank crouched down and began looking for something in the pack. "If we don't do something fast, we're done for." He stood up, holding one of the emergency flares the bear had graciously left behind. "Hopefully this will slow Stinky down."

I grinned. "Nice thinking."

He ran a few yards back down the tunnel, lit the flare, and tossed it as far as he could. A thick cloud of smoke instantly filled the back of the cave. All that smoke in such a confined space would definitely leave our pursuer coughing, and might even force whoever it was back until it cleared.

I lay on my stomach, stuck my head out of the cave entrance, and peered down. Heights don't usually bother me, but looking down at the jagged rocks in the canyon far below made my head spin. I took a deep breath to center myself and studied the cliff, looking for an alternate way down that didn't involve plunging to our doom.

There was no way to see it standing up, but from my stomach, I could tell that the cliff face didn't drop straight down from the cave. The lip of the cave jutted out a few feet like a little awning over a narrow ledge hidden behind the vines about ten feet below. If we could get down to it, we might be able to find another route off the cliff. Or at least maybe a place to hide. Only there was no way to climb down from where we were—not with the rope Aleksei had tied to the piton at the mouth of the cave ripped away—and trying to jump onto a two-foot-wide ledge of rock from a story up definitely wasn't an option.

"There's a small ledge down there. If we can get down to it, we might have a chance." I stared at the torn bit of rope and groaned. We'd had plenty of rope we could have replaced it with, but— "The rope was in the pack the bear took, wasn't it?"

"Have I mentioned that I really hate that bear?" Frank asked in return, confirming my suspicion.

I was pushing myself back to my feet when I noticed

the paracord survival bracelet on my wrist. I wasn't used to wearing it and had almost forgotten it was there!

"Thank you, Last Chance General Store!" I said, unraveling the bracelet as quickly as I could. "There should be just enough cord in here for us to lower ourselves down."

I popped the clasp with the little compass into my pocket for safekeeping and went to work securing the paracord to the piton with a knot. I tied the other end to our remaining pack to turn it into a makeshift harness.

Luckily, Frank and I had lots of experience tying knots over the years, because you never knew when a good knot might help you out of a bad spot. And we were in a bad spot for sure. I could hear Stinky coughing somewhere farther inside the cave, and the sound was growing closer. The smoke screen from Frank's flare had slowed our pursuer down, but it hadn't stopped them.

Normally a daring drop from a cliff face onto a narrow ledge ten feet below would require a bunch of safety gear. We wouldn't have had time for it even if we'd had the gear. This was one of those absolute-last-resort, definitely-don't-try-this-at-home-unless-there's-a-real-life-gun-toting-villain-chasing-you-type situations. Why was it my bro and I seemed to get ourselves into so many of those? That was an unsolved mystery for another day. Just then it was time to drop off a cliff.

Frank went first.

"I can't believe I'm actually doing this," he moaned, taking a deep breath and dropping himself over the side.

He fell from sight, and for a terrifying moment I didn't know whether he'd made it. From the grunting and muttering to himself that followed, I knew he had.

"Aleksei put handholds down here to grab onto," he called back just loud enough above a whisper that I could hear him and hopefully whoever's feet I heard stomping toward me through the cave couldn't. "It's not too bad."

He gave the rope a tug, and I yanked the pack back up and slipped it on. I did two last things before following Frank over the side. I covered the piton and the first few feet of paracord with vines to hide them. Then I screamed.

The scream wasn't out of fear—although, I'm not going to lie, I was a little afraid; I mean, who wouldn't be? But with a little luck, our perp would hear the scream, then see the parachute in the trees on the other side of the canyon and assume we'd been the ones to jump with parachutes. I even let the volume of my scream trail off to mimic the Doppler effect of my voice getting farther away so they'd think I was actually falling. That was my plan, at least. Because if our pursuer saw the cord and got down on their bellies like I had, they'd realize there were a couple of Hardy-boy-size sitting ducks hiding ten feet below them.

I steadied myself on the ledge next to Frank, grabbing onto the metal rings Aleksei had hammered into the rock every few feet as handholds, and pressed myself as close to the rock wall as I could. Just below the tips of our toes was the sheer drop into the canyon. Just over our heads was an armed criminal who'd proven they weren't above using lethal tactics.

A moment later the sound of coughing and the smell of skunk reached the mouth of the cave. Pebbles trickled over the edge and rained down on us as the perp's feet dislodged debris from the edge. There was the bright glint of sunlight hitting glass above us. If everything was going according to plan, the glass was from the perp's binoculars, and he or she was staring down at the parachute, assuming we'd jumped.

It was when I saw the steel muzzle poke out from the cave's entrance above us that I realized it wasn't binoculars the perp was looking out of. It was the scope of a hunting rifle. But it wasn't until the barrel started to lower toward us that I got really nervous.

ON THE PROWL

10

FRANK

I **RESISTED THE URGE TO GASP AS THE RIFLE** barrel angled toward us. I did my best not to even breathe. Our stalker was a mere ten feet above our heads, armed and dangerous. Did they know we were there? We were about to find out.

Just as the muzzle started to point straight down, the perp muttered in frustration and withdrew the gun back into the cave. It had worked!

A barrage of small rocks showered past us as the perp kicked at the dirt on the cave floor. There was a crackle of static and then the sound of our pursuer's voice retreating as they talked into what must have been a two-way radio. The wind had picked up, dampening the sound, and there was no way to tell what they were saying, or even if it was a man or a woman. All I was able to hear were a few fragmented words.

"... *jammed up*... *not working*... *got away*."

And then silence. Our plan had worked! Now we just had to find a way down without falling.

"This way," Joe whispered. "Aleksei has more spikes driven into the rocks. The down climb is going to be dangerous, but I think we can make it."

"Is anything around here *not* dangerous?" I asked, carefully following my brother down the rocky cliff. Luckily, we only had to descend another ten or fifteen feet before we reached a wider ledge. And this one led to an actual path down into the canyon.

"Finally, a break!" I exclaimed. I looked back up the cliff. The cave was now hidden from sight. which meant anyone still lurking up there wouldn't be able to see us, either.

The path Joe found was still dicey, but it sure beat trying to climb off the cliff in reverse without any safety gear. We crossed the canyon floor as quickly as we could, running between boulders and patches of thick brush to keep ourselves hidden. The stream running through the middle was pretty low, so crossing wasn't too hard.

Soon we were staring up at the parachute Dr. Kroopnik must have used to leap from the cave. Whether he'd leaped safely remained to be seen. Judging from the way the parachute was tangled in the trees, the landing hadn't been a smooth one.

"That cliff may seem high to us, but for a BASE jumper, it's dangerously low," Joe observed. BASE jumping is like skydiving, only you leap from a fixed object like a cliff or building top instead of an aircraft—the exact kind of extreme sport I had no interest in trying. "It's super risky even in ideal conditions. It's a miracle he made it at all."

"He must have gotten tangled up and had to cut himself down," I surmised. I looked from the parachute's severed cords to the rocks on the ground below. That was when I saw the drops of blood. "I think he's hurt, Joe."

Joe nodded solemnly. "The tracks look like he was dragging his bad leg a lot worse than usual. He left a clear trail of prints in the mud. It should be easy to follow."

The tracks led us down the canyon and onto a game trail back through the forest. Following the prints might have been difficult for an amateur, but this wasn't the first time Joe and I had tracked someone through the woods. There were more trees and less brush, making Dr. K's escape route easier for us to follow than it would have been in the thick brush we'd had to whack through to get to the cabin.

We'd followed the trail for about a mile through the woods when Joe suddenly froze in place on the path in front of me.

"Please tell me that's just from a really large kitty cat," he said, staring straight down at the ground.

I knelt to look at the huge feline paw print stamped in

the forest floor next to Joe's boot. "Um, do you consider mountain lions kitties?"

"That's what I was afraid of." He looked around nervously. "We may not be the only ones tracking Dr. K."

"Dr. K's been studying them, so we know they've been in the area," I said. A chill ran down my spine. The naturalist in me was buzzing with excitement. The rest of me was terrified.

The mountain lion. Scientific name *Puma concolor*, aka the puma, panther, cougar, catamount, or ghost cat, depending on who you ask. They're not technically lions and don't have the regal manes of their larger African relatives, but they're one of the most elusive and fiercest predators in North America. A full-grown male can top nine feet long nose to tail and weigh over two hundred pounds. They might not be larger than black bears, but they're often even deadlier hunters. Black bears are omnivores, and a lot of their diet comes from fruit, berries, nuts, and grubs. They don't actually hunt large game like full-grown deer all that often. Mountain lions? They are pure carnivores, and large prey like deer is their favorite delicacy.

The huge paw print Joe had spotted verified the premise of Dr. Kroopnik's research and was important evidence in his quest to document the presence of a viable northeastern mountain lion population. It was a thrilling discovery—or it would have been if I hadn't suspected it might be stalking a friend of ours. We still didn't know why Dr. K had run off with Aleksei's garnets, but even if he had stolen them for himself, I wanted the law to bring him to justice. Not a hungry mountain lion!

Normally, there would be nothing to be afraid of. You're more likely to get hit by lightning than attacked by a mountain They *almost never* pose a threat to humans except in unusual situations when the animals are sick or starving—and from the thriving ecosystem on Black Bear Mountain, there was plenty of natural prey. Scientists don't usually fall into the category of natural mountain lion entrées—but if that scientist was wounded? Apex predators may hunt weak or injured animals to conserve energy. Could a hungry cougar have caught a whiff of Dr. K's blood and be contemplating him as a dinner option?

And even if two healthy teenagers like Joe and me might not normally tempt a mountain lion's taste buds, it's never smart to let your guard down if you cross paths with one of the most formidable predators in America. I would *never* intentionally harm an animal like that, but I sure would try to chase one away if it threatened us. Joe tightened his grip on the hatchet, and I picked up the heftiest stick I saw.

We crept along quietly until we saw the trail disappear behind a large boulder a few yards ahead. Joe looked back at me. I knew what he was thinking. A boulder like that would make a great ambush spot for somebody. Or some*thing*. He gave me a hand signal to follow him off the trail and circle around. I had just given him the thumbs-up when we heard something rustle behind the boulder.

We both froze. Whatever made that sound was a lot larger than a squirrel or a skunk. What we heard next could only have come from one creature. It was the bloodcurdling yowl of a mountain lion.

I grabbed onto Joe's arm to make sure he stood his ground in case he had the same impulse that I did—to run! It sure was tempting, but I also knew that was just about the last thing we should do. Running from a large predator can remind them of prey and trigger their hunting instincts. When faced with a large, aggressive animal like a bear or mountain lion, you're supposed to stand up tall, wave your arms around, and yell to make yourself seem as big and intimidating as you can. We'd done the same thing when confronted by a large black bear on our last trip, and it had worked. Would it scare off a mountain lion? I didn't know, but we didn't have much choice except to try.

We held our breath, waiting to see if the animal would show itself. There was another rustle, and then the creature emerged. It had a terrifying muzzle, all right, only this one didn't have fangs. We were staring down the barrel of a tranquilizer gun.

ENDANGERED SPECIES

11

JOE

MY FEAR VANISHED AS I LOOKED from the tranquilizer gun to the guy holding it. We were going to have better luck reasoning with him than a with mountain lion, that was for sure.

"Frank?! Joe?!" The gun dropped to the scientist's side as Max Kroopnik ran over to embrace us. Actually, limped over was more like it. It was clear he'd reinjured his left leg badly. "You're the last people I expected to see!"

"You haven't been eaten by a mountain lion!" Frank exclaimed, hugging him back.

"I about feel like it," he said, looking down at his tattered, bloody clothes.

"That's one heck of a wildcat impression you got there,

Doc. I thought for sure we were about to get pounced on," I told him.

"The idea was to scare whoever it was away, not actually eat them." He grinned and limped back behind the boulder, using the large rock to prop himself up. We followed him as he reached down into a bundle of gear, pulled out a digital recorder, and pressed play.

"*YOWWWWLLL!*" it growled.

"Field recordings I made of a large male I've been monitoring. I'd hoped it would chase off whoever's been after me. I just didn't expect it to be you two."

"Technically, I guess you could say we have been tracking you, but we're not *after* you," I said. "At least we weren't at first. We came to Black Bear Mountain to make sure you were okay."

"Aleksei sent us a letter from prison saying he hadn't heard from you and was worried something had happened," Frank explained.

Max smiled. "I can always count on Aleksei. How is the big guy doing?"

"Um, okay I guess, besides being in prison and worrying about you," I replied, looking at the bedraggled scientist. "He said you'd written that there were suspicious people snooping around the mountain. Then when he didn't get another letter five or six weeks later like usual, he wrote to us and asked us to check on you."

"I've had the sense for a few months now that people are

following me around the mountain," he confirmed. "That's odd that he didn't get my last letter, though. I haven't been to town, but I handed a letter for Aleksei and a couple others off to Dan to mail for me when he stopped by on one of his trips up with some hikers."

"Dan sure has a knack for turning up around here at convenient times," said Frank.

"Or *in*convenient, if you're the one trying not to get crushed by a tree or to send a letter. Do you think he intercept—"

"Wait, you said you weren't the ones after me *at first*. What does that mean?" Max cut me off, limping back a step and tightening his grip on the tranquilizer gun at his side.

"We know you took Aleksei's garnets, Dr. K," Frank said, his voice sympathetic but firm. Dr. K was our friend, but he was also a suspect. Which seemed to come as news to him.

"You think I'd steal from my best friend?!" he asked incredulously.

"I'm sorry, Doc," I said. "We're not saying you did it. We just think it's possible. All the clues point to you taking the garnets from Aleksei's hideout, and until we can rule out theft, we have to consider you a suspect."

"It's a working hypothesis," Frank explained.

Dr. K gawked at us. "Aleksei told you he thought I was in trouble. What do you think? I destroyed my own lab and nearly killed myself jumping off a cliff as part of a robbery ploy?"

I shrugged. "Stranger things have happened around here. I mean, Aleksei did crash a plane to fake his death and spend the next thirty years pretending to be a mythical man-eating mountain man," I reminded him.

"I'll admit, I did get some wacky ideas from Aleksei, but staging my own disappearance wasn't one of them. I just wanted to keep the garnets safe from whoever *is* trying to steal them." He reached into his pants pocket and pulled out a plastic specimen bag, the kind scientists use to pick up interesting things they find in the field, like bits of animal hair or funky mushrooms and whatever other weird stuff scientists find interesting. Only it wasn't fur or toadstools in this one. The bag was full of radiant green demantoid garnets.

He placed the bag in Frank's hand. "So you know I'm telling the truth. You can probably keep them safer than me now anyway."

Our eyes stayed fixed on the bag as Max slid his body down the boulder with a groan and took a seat on the ground. The garnets ranged from the size of a Ping-Pong ball—which we knew from experience was *HUGE* for a gem this rare—to tiny pebbles, but even the pebbles were gorgeous.

"I used to dream of finding one of these when I collected rocks as a kid," Frank said in awe, eyes fixed on the largest stone. "But I never could have imagined finding any this big."

"Aleksei calls them Siberian emeralds," Max said as he massaged his bad leg. "There might be only a handful of them in the entire world, and probably no one except Aleksei has found one in nearly a century."

I knew from last time that demantoids were one of the rarest precious gems in the world, and the best ones are found almost exclusively in one part of Russia—the Ural Mountains, where Aleksei was from. It wasn't just the rarity that made demantoids so valuable either. The transparent gemstones were green on the surface, but green was only the beginning.

"'Demantoid' is derived from the French word for 'diamond,'" Frank said reverently. "But these refract even *more* light than diamonds do."

The clouds parted as Frank held up the bag and rays of sunshine burst into the forest, hitting the stones and sending a brilliant rainbow sparkling over us. I'd seen some on our last trip too, but I still couldn't stop marveling at the gems and the way they put on a zillion-color light show when the sun hit them just so. It was like Frank was holding a bag full of mini magic disco balls in the palm of his hand.

"Something else, aren't they? The beauty and intricacy of nature never cease to amaze me," Max said, looking up at the stones from his seat on the ground. "I'm not trying to profit off them. I'm trying to protect them."

His words snapped me out of my demantoid daze. I wanted to believe Max. Badly. But I couldn't entirely rule him out as a suspect until we had more information. "From who?"

"I wish I knew," he sighed. "I was on my way back late at night after checking my trail cameras for mountain lion activity when I realized there was someone in my research station."

"What did they look like?" Frank urged.

"I didn't get close enough to find out," Max said, sounding a little embarrassed. "I was still on the other side of the bridge when I saw the flashlight moving around. It was too dark to make out much more than shadows from that distance. And after what happened to me last time someone snuck in, I wasn't about to take any chances. I'm afraid I'm not as courageous as you boys."

"There's nothing to feel bad about, Doc," I tried to reassure him. "Having someone stuff you in you in a cabinet and steal your identity tends to leave an impression."

"And I know for a fact how brave you are," Frank added. "I wasn't alone on that raft when it went over the falls."

"Yeah, and you do spend your free time chasing after mountain lions," I said. "But just because we think you're brave doesn't mean you're off the hook yet. What happened next?"

"Once I saw whoever it was tearing the place apart, I figured they had to be after the garnets," he continued. "The press our last little adventure got brought all kinds of thrill seekers and treasure hunters out of the woodwork. They usually just stomp around and make a mess of the woods. I don't know how many times I've had to clean up after them. This was the first time one of them had the audacity to ignore the *no trespassing* signs I had to put up and actually break in."

"He wasn't a big, military-looking dude with a crew cut, was he?" I asked, recalling the description we'd received of the treasure hunter calling himself John Smith.

"I tried looking through my binoculars, but the person was dressed in black and wearing a face mask. They might have been kind of big, maybe. I couldn't really tell much from that angle."

"Do you think it could have been Drawes?" asked Frank.

"Drawes," Dr. K spat. "I wouldn't put it past him. Whoever it was, they were turning the place upside down looking for something. I hate to think of all the damage they did to my research, but all the equipment is insured. The garnets sure aren't, though." He looked at the baggie with the demantoids. "Aleksei showed me where he'd hidden the final stash. The only thing I could think to do was go to the cabin and get them before the burglar could. I'd planned to get the garnets, sleep at the cabin, and get out early the next morning, only . . ." He paused, giving a pained look at his bad leg.

"Only . . . ?" I prompted.

"Only the trapdoor in the fireplace jammed and I couldn't get it back open from the inside. I'd trapped myself in Aleksei's secret bunker."

"A bunker with only one other exit," Frank said.

"Aleksei had stocked the cave with food, but all the

water jugs had frozen and burst over the winter while he was in prison. It had never occurred to me to replace them. I never figured *I'd* need a secret hideout. I only had enough water on me to ration for a few days, and then . . ." He gave a little shudder.

"You jumped."

"It was the same parachute Aleksei used to bail out when he crashed his plane here to fake his death in the 1980s. I didn't even know if it still worked," Max said, cringing. "He kept it in the cave as a backup escape plan if the authorities ever cornered him. He figured he could take out the piton he'd put in the entrance so no one could climb down after him, then take a flying leap to safety. I told him it was a ridiculous plan. He just gave me that wild smile and reminded me that it had been a ridiculous plan involving a parachute that had kept him out of prison for three decades."

"I like the way the big guy thinks," I said, earning dubious looks from Frank and Max, who shook his head and continued.

"I would have just used the rope to climb down—that would have been dangerous enough as it was—but the darn thing had rotted away. I put it off for as long as I could until my water ran out. Without water, well, I didn't know what my odds were of surviving a low-altitude BASE jump with a repacked, vintage parachute, but I figured they were at least better than zero. So I strapped the thing on, got a running start, and . . ." Dr. K pantomimed leaping off the cliff with his hand. "It's a miracle I survived. I did bang up my bad leg something fierce when I hit that tree, though."

Max rapped his knuckles gently against the boulder. "I've been hiding out here for a few days, trying to nurse myself back to health so I could make the hike out. It's not the ritziest hospital room, but I've got good cover, easy access to the creek to boil fresh water, and wild edible plants and medicines all around me."

"Good job staying positive, Dr. K," Frank complimented him. We both knew from our wilderness training that keeping your spirits up was one of the most important things you could do in a survival situation. They didn't cover this in wilderness boot camp, but one of the *other* most important things is not getting caught by a skunky-smelling, gun-wielding gem thief.

"If the trapdoor into Aleksei's bunker jammed behind you, maybe whoever followed us into the cave got stuck as well," I said hopefully.

"You didn't see who it was either, huh?" Max asked.

Frank and I shook our heads.

"You're the only one who's had a visual on the suspect," said Frank.

"I'm not the only one, actually. I don't think it will do much good because the image is barely more than a shadow, but one of the trail cams I set up to monitor mountain lions picked up something over near Aleksei's old crash site. This is from a week before I saw my research station getting ransacked." Dr.

K rummaged through his pack as he spoke. "At first I thought it was just a hiker, but I'm not so sure anymore."

Frank and I hunched down over his shoulders as he pulled out a digital viewer and started fast-forwarding through clips of wildlife passing by a fallen log in the woods.

"I keep trail cameras strapped to trees in cougar-friendly habitats throughout the mountain range. Every time an animal passes within the field of the camera's motion sensors, it takes a short video clip. I'd been out in the field for over a week collecting the memory cards. Didn't get any mountain lion footage this time, but I did get this—"

Three more clips of a coyote, a porcupine, and a raccoon flew across the little screen in fast-forward before he hit the play button. The screen was static for a moment, and then a creature's silhouette passed by through the woods just at the edge of the frame. The clip barely lasted a second, and it was impossible to make out any detail, but one thing was certain: this creature walked on two feet.

"So either that's Bigfoot, or you may have caught a shot of the perp," I said. "Can you pause and zoom in?"

It didn't do much good. The person was at the very edge of the motion sensor's range, with their back to the camera *and* obscured by trees. The way they were positioned, it was hard to even get a sense of scale to know how tall they were. It didn't help that the camera captured the shot in fading evening light. The only real detail you could make out was the faint pattern of camouflage on their clothing.

"The camo could point to the description we received for John Smith," Frank suggested. "Lots of people wear camouflage in the woods, though."

"And it could just be a hiker like Dr. K first thought," I said, frustrated at what looked like another dead end. "Can you play it again?"

"The controls on this aren't very precise, so it may take me a second to get back to the right spot," Max said, hitting rewind.

The blurry suspect blurred by in reverse and out of frame. There was a short blip of blank screen before the raccoon sped backward toward the camera, appeared to stop for a few frames to sniff the lens, then zipped out of the picture.

"Oops, went too far," Dr. K said, hitting the play button. "I get a lot of raccoon shots. They're about as ubiquitous as mountain lions are rare. That curious little guy stopped by just a minute or two before the person in camo. The video will skip right ahead once it passes."

The raccoon ambled toward the lens in regular speed, gave it a few sniffs, then moseyed off along the trail.

And that's when Frank's and my mouths dropped open. Sure, raccoons may be a dime a dozen in the woods, but raccoons with perfectly round bald patches on their read ends? They tend to be a whole lot rarer.

SHOWDOWN AT HIGH RACCOON

12

FRANK

"HEY, I KNOW THAT RACCOON!" DR. KROOPNIK blurted.

"Ricky," Joe snarled.

"I don't think it's a coincidence Ken and Cherry Fritwell's pet raccoon is running around Black Bear Mountain," I said.

"And I don't think that little jerky thief is flying solo, either," Joe surmised. "The only reason that trash panda would show up all the way out here is if someone brought him."

Max looked flabbergasted. "You think Ken and Cherry have something do with this? But I've known them for years."

"They aren't the only ones cozy with that raccoon. Cherry told us that it was the lodge that rescued him first. They said Ricky still goes out there for playdates with Dan and—"

"Steven," Dr. K grunted. "I haven't trusted that guy since he helped Casey's no-good sister try to steal Aleksei's garnets the first time."

"Steven's supposed to be out of town, but that could just be a convenient alibi to give him cover," I speculated.

"Speaking of alibis, we don't have any proof that Dan was really booked by other guests and didn't just ditch us so he could follow us to the garnets," said Joe.

"With his guide skills, he could have tracked us easily enough," I said. "He also had the opportunity to bear-bait our pack with honey and set us up to be smashed by that falling tree on the ATV ride in."

Max looked at us wide-eyed. "Sounds like your trip here has been almost as calamitous as mine."

"Someone is dead set on getting those garnets for themselves. It could be any of the people on our suspect list, or all of them, for all we know," Joe said.

"There could be someone else at the lodge or another local with a connection to Ricky that we don't know about too," I pointed out. "The best way to find out is to start asking."

"And the best way to do that is to get back to civilization and switch from survival mode to interrogation mode." Joe looked down at Max. "What do you think, Doc? Can you walk out of here?"

"I don't think I'd make it more than a couple miles on this bum leg, and if someone is tracking us, it's going to be easy to catch up to me hobbling down the mountain.

No, I don't think I can walk all the way out." Dr. K's words sounded bleak, but the grin on his lips didn't match what he'd just said. "But I can fly."

"Hate to break it to you, Doc," Joe said. "The chopper's out of commission. Someone tore open the control panel and smashed the radio."

"They must have destroyed the radio after I left, but they're not the ones who tampered with the controls," he said, still grinning. "When I realized someone was following me, I decided to make the helicopter my last resort, in case I needed an escape. So I made it look like the helicopter was out of commission so no one could destroy it and take away my chance of safety. It will only take me a few minutes to put the fuse back in and reconnect the wires."

"Quick thinking, Dr. K!"

"Thanks, Frank. If I hadn't gotten trapped in the cave under Aleksei's cabin, I would have doubled back and flown to town with the garnets. That plan went out the window when I went out the cave door and busted my leg. I don't think I can make it back up to the top of the mountain on my own in this condition—but I bet I can with your help."

I offered him my hand. "Then let's get team Hardy-Kroopnik in gear!"

"Copy that," Joe confirmed, grabbing Dr. K's pack as I helped him back to his feet.

We moved out single file with Joe in the lead, Dr. K limping along with a walking stick, and me bringing up the rear.

We hadn't made it far when a familiar voice drifted down to us from farther up the hill. We all came to an instant halt. The voice was familiar, but it wasn't human. It was raccoon.

"Ricky," Joe whispered angrily as the *rick-rick-rick-rick* of the raccoon's signature chatter grew closer. "You'd better get that tranquilizer gun ready, Doc."

"We can't use this on a raccoon, Joe," he whispered back. "There's enough sedative in there to put a full-grown mountain lion to sleep so I can fit it with a radio collar."

"Good, then it should do the trick on whoever Ricky Raccoon brought with him," Joe replied, tightening the grip on his hatchet. "Hopefully we won't have to use it, but whoever followed us into the cave was armed, and we're not leaving you alone, so running isn't an option. If we can get the drop on them, maybe we can make them take a nap before anyone gets hurt for real."

Dr. Kroopnik nodded reluctantly. Nervous beads of sweat dotted his brow, but he didn't back down. And neither did I.

I scanned the woody hill ahead of us. Whoever was up there had the high ground. The only advantage we might have would be surprise—*if* we saw them before they saw us.

"We'd better take cover behind those trees," I whispered. "Maybe we can catch them in an ambush."

We had just begun to move off the trail when another voice boomed out from up the hill. This one didn't sound human either. It sounded *demonic*.

"Take one more step, and none of you leave this mountain alive."

I gulped as a figure stepped out from behind a large maple tree. There'd been an ambush, all right—and we'd been the ones to walk right into it. The assailant wore camo like the perp on Dr. K's trail cam, only now we could see the rest of him clearly too. Not that it helped me identify him. Half his face was hidden by an enormous, unkempt beard. The features I could see were large and exaggerated, almost like a Neanderthal's. A bushy bearskin hat sat atop his head. In his hands were a pair of Old West–style six-shooters.

It was as if the mythical man-eating wild man Aleksei had once pretended to be had come to life for real.

MASKED MAYHEM

13

JOE

DROP IT, DR. DOOM," THE GUNMAN commanded Dr. K. "Or should I say Dr. *Doomed*."

He let out a fiendish laugh. His voice was unnaturally deep and electronic, like the way people in witness protection sound on true crime shows when the producers change their voices and stick them in the shadows to hide their identities. I had a pretty good hunch it wasn't the gunman's real voice either. He or she had to be using one of the small, portable voice changers spy shops sell online.

His voice wasn't all he was hiding. Once the initial shock at his appearance wore off and I took a closer look at his face, I could tell he was wearing a mask and fake beard. It was like he was a parody of Aleksei's wild mountain man legend. Only unlike Aleksei, this wild man meant us harm.

I couldn't tell who the perp behind the fake face and voice was. I just knew it wasn't the same one who'd broken into Dr. K's station and chased us through the cave. Because this one didn't reek of skunk. The question was, were Beard Face and Stinky partners, or was there more than one would-be gem thief on the loose on Black Bear Mountain?

I could tell from how tightly Dr. K was gripping his tranquilizer gun that he was more worried about Beard Face's revolver than his identity.

"You've got one shot of a low-velocity dart that you'll have to shoot uphill." It seems Beard Face had noticed the tranquilizer gun as well. "I've got the high ground and twelve high-powered slugs to go with it. Think you can hit me with that little pop gun of yours before I put lead into both your friends here?"

I hated to admit it, but he was right. We'd been outmaneuvered.

"He's got the drop on us, Doc. Better do as he says," I told Max.

The features of his mask didn't change, but I could hear the smile in his mechanized voice. "You can call me the Ghost of the Wild Man."

"Aleksei wasn't a coward who pointed guns at teenagers," Max shot back.

"Shut up and throw me the garnets," Beard Face snapped. "I know you've got them."

"I don't know what you're talking about," Max bluffed, his voice shaking.

Beard Face cocked the hammers on both guns. "You can give them to me voluntarily, or I can take them off you."

There was an earsplitting *BANG* as his right trigger finger twitched. Splinters of wood erupted from the tree two feet to Max's left. I didn't know who the self-proclaimed Ghost of the Wild Man was, but he wasn't shooting ghost bullets.

Frank looked at me. I didn't want to, but I nodded. The gems were valuable, but not as valuable as our lives. Frank pulled the bag with the demantoids from his pocket.

"Come and get them," he said.

My heart pounded inside my chest. If we could lure Beard Face close enough, we might get an opening to disarm him.

"Nice try, kid. You're gonna toss them on the ground for the raccoon," commanded the mechanized voice.

Frank gritted his teeth. And then did what the gunman said.

"Fetch, Ricky."

The raccoon didn't seem particularly thrown by the voice changer and scurried down the hill. I sneered at the varmint as it snatched the baggie in its teeth. First my trail mix, then my jerky, now Aleksei's garnets. This furry little masked thief was really getting on my nerves. Ricky must have known what I was thinking, because he hissed in my direction on his way back up the hill. I hissed back.

Ricky's master holstered one of his pistols, took the bag from Ricky, and held it up to the light. Sparkles of brilliance and color washed over them. "At last! The cannibal's gems are ours!"

"Aleksei's not a cannibal. If anyone on this mountain is a monster, it's you," Max shouted.

Beard Face took a few steps closer and tossed three double-looped plastic zip ties on the ground. They were the same kind police sometimes use as disposable handcuffs.

"Help each other cuff your hands behind your backs."

"You're going to have to make us," I said.

Beard Face nodded at the fresh bullet hole in the tree next to Max and cocked the hammer on the pistol a second time. "I don't want to hurt you, but I will."

Max put a gentle hand on my shoulder. "Let's do what he says, boys. I can't stand the idea of you coming out here to help me and getting badly hurt because of it."

If looks were laser beams, I would have zapped Beard Face right off the mountain. They're not, though, so we were stuck doing what he ordered. I intentionally left Frank's cuffs a little loose to give us a fighting chance at escape, and I had a feeling he'd done the same to Max. Beard Face was a step ahead of us, though, tightening each tie once our hands were zipped behind our backs.

"Now each of you take a seat with your backs to that big tree," he ordered, jamming a pistol into Dr. K's side to let us know he wasn't going to take no for an answer.

"You can't just leave us here in the middle of the wilderness cuffed to a tree without food or water," Frank said as Beard Face tied us to the tree with a length of rope.

"You brought this on yourselves by meddling." Beard Face gave the knot an extra yank to tighten it, then patted the butt of each pistol. "Glad you didn't make me use these. I hate violence."

It sounded so ridiculous coming out of Beard Face's mouth, I couldn't help laughing. "You could have fooled us. Since we got here, we've been assaulted with a tree, turned into bear bait, chased off a cliff, shot at, and tied up at gunpoint."

"Necessary evils," Beard Face replied. "When we found out the famous Hardy boys were coming to help Kroopnik, we had to put contingency plans in motion to stop you from snooping around."

The "we" confirmed what I already suspected: Beard Face wasn't acting alone.

"Are you and your stinky partner so scared of a couple of teenagers that you have to hide behind a phony voice and a ridiculous mask?" I snapped.

"This ridiculous disguise of mine is what's keeping you alive. Being tied to a tree is better than being buried under one, which would have been the alternative if you'd seen my face."

So much for my plan to bait the perp into giving up his identity. For the time being, it looked like solving the mystery might mean burying the detectives.

"As long as you sit tight and don't try anything funny while I make my getaway, I'll even call in a tip that you're here," Beard Face said, starting back up the hill.

"How thoughtful of you," Frank hissed. "You're practically a hero."

Beard Face ignored his sarcasm. "Always did have a soft spot for helpless woodland creatures. Come on, Ricky. We're gonna be rich." Our perp turned his back to us one last time before disappearing from view. "Just try not to get yourselves eaten by anything while we're gone."

LIVE BAIT

14

FRANK

THE SO-CALLED GHOST OF THE WILD Man stomped out of sight through the woods. The last thing we heard was the crackle of the two-way radio clicking to life and the mechanized voice saying something into it. He was moving fast and the wind had picked up, making it hard to decipher, but it sounded kind of like, "Rendezvous time. On . . . way . . . way. Get ready . . . take off." Some of the words were garbled, but him telling his accomplice to get ready to leave the mountain made sense now that they had what they'd come for.

Not that it did us much good, tied to a tree and totally at the mercy of the wilderness. And, judging from the giant paw prints we'd seen while tracking Dr. Kroopnik, that included a very large mountain lion. Attacks on humans may be rare, but what would an apex predator do if it came across three slabs of live steak tied to a maple tree like a giant shish kebab? It was one animal behavior field study I'm pretty sure no one had ever conducted, and I wasn't thrilled about us being the test subjects.

"I really hate that raccoon," Joe griped. "And Beard Face is a close second."

"The detective in me wants to break this down and figure out who's behind that mask, but I think getting out of here has to be our priority. Knowing whodunit won't do us any good if we never make it off this mountain," I said.

"I for one don't trust him to keep his promise to call for help," Joe said.

"Even if he does, it could be too late by the time the rescuers find us," fretted Max. "We'll be lucky to make it even four days without water."

"Four days? At the rate these bugs are eating me, there won't be anything left in two," Joe said as he tried to blow a mosquito off his cheek. "Ow!"

"The zip ties are too tight to squeeze out of, but if I can reach deep enough into my pocket, I might be able to get my Swiss Army knife."

I strained to twist my arms around so my hands had access to my front pocket. The plastic zip tie cut painfully into my wrist, but I didn't let it stop me. I was able to slide my fingers into my pocket just deep enough to touch the knife with a fingertip. So close. Not close enough. I had to try a different strategy. I pinched the seam of my pocket between my fingertips and tried to yank my pants pocket around so I could reach farther inside. "Almost . . . Got it!"

"Way to go, bro!" Joe cheered.

"Now I just have to get the blade or the saw open with my hands cuffed together behind my back," I said. "Without dropping it or cutting myself."

It was a tall order. I took a deep breath and reminded myself that if I wasn't careful, this situation could get a lot worse. A cut back home—where you can easily wash your finger and grab some antibiotic ointment and a Band-Aid—is no big deal. In the middle of a remote wilderness with no way to clean or bandage it to stop the bleeding and prevent infection, it could turn deadly.

I did my best to tune out the world around me and just focus. I was so focused I almost didn't hear Joe when he spoke.

"Dude . . . Dude!" he urged in a hushed voice. "I don't want to rush you, but you might want to hurry up. I think there's something out there."

Then I heard it too. Dead leaves crunching under a creature's feet. And whatever was out there, it wasn't a small animal.

"Maybe the gunman's come back to shoot us after all," Dr. K whimpered.

"Or maybe one of your mountain lions wants to sample some people jerky," Joe suggested bleakly.

I did my best to ignore my heart pounding in my chest as I gripped the knife in my left hand and tried to pinch one of the blades open with the fingers of my right.

"It's open!" I whispered. "It's . . ."

It was the wrong blade was what it was.

Joe twisted his head around to look. "Bro, I think this is one mystery that detecting tool isn't going to help us solve."

I'd accidentally opened the magnifying glass instead of the knife!

CRUNCH.

Another footstep on dead leaves. Whatever was stalking us was only a few yards away, close enough to burst out of the woods and strike. There'd be no running this time. No fighting. Not unless I got free. Our only hope literally rested in my bound hands.

I frantically tried to feel for the right blade. But even if I got it open, I'd still have to somehow reposition the knife upside down with the blade facing outward and try to cut through the plastic. It was a delicate operation that required time, and time was something we had just run out of.

My mouth dropped open as our stalker stepped into view. This creature wasn't a mountain lion and definitely didn't have a beard.

"Jones!" I cried.

A ROCKY REUNION

15

JOE

"FRANK! JOE! YOU'RE ALIVE!" JONES shouted.

She rushed out of the woods, dropped her pack and the GPS device she was holding, took out a pocketknife, and went straight to work cutting away the rope binding us to the tree.

"I'm even happier to see you now than usual," Frank gushed as the rope fell away.

Jones managed to blush mid-rescue, though it was a little hard to tell. Her face was still red, puffy, and hive-speckled from yesterday's allergic reaction. She was a shy, puffy-faced action heroine!

"You're not a villain!" I blurted as she sliced the zip tie off Frank's wrists and looked at me like I'd lost it.

"What are you talking about, Joe? Of course I'm not."

"It was, um, just a working theory," I said sheepishly.

"I told you." Frank rolled his eyes at me and gave Jones a huge, grateful hug. "My younger and definitely not wiser brother thought you might have spiked your own iced tea with an allergen as part of a wacky ploy to steal the garnets for yourself."

This time it was me who blushed. From embarrassment. "I'm sorry, Jones. I didn't really think you did it. We were just struggling to come up with logical suspects, and, well, I never should have doubted you. Um, could you uncuff me now?"

"Hmm . . ." She tapped her knife against her thigh like she was contemplating what I'd asked, then grinned and cut me loose. "How many times do I have to save your skin before you just admit I'm as good of a detective as you?"

"Um, maybe three or four more times," I suggested.

Jones gave me a playful shove and followed it with a hug. She sliced the cuffs off Max next. "Nice to meet you, Dr. Kroopnik. Frank told me a ton of good things about you and all the great research you're doing."

"And I'll get to do more of it now, thanks to you," he said, rubbing his wrists where the plastic had cut into the skin. "I thought we were goners this time for sure."

"I did too," Jones admitted. "When I saw the GPS tracker stop moving, I feared the worst."

"The GPS what?!" Frank and I blurted.

Jones looked down at my wrist, where the paracord survival bracelet Cherry had given me used to be. "Do you still have the survival bracelet with the compass on it?"

"I have the compass," I said, reaching into my pocket. "The bracelet saved our hides earlier today when one of the perps chased us off a cliff."

"Yeah, well, I think it's also what led them to you in the first place," she said, taking the compass from me and holding it up. "Because this thing has a tracking device hidden inside it."

"It what?!" Frank and I blurted again.

I shook my head in disgust. "I've been a walking perp magnet. No wonder they kept finding us so easily."

Dr. K looked stricken. "Cherry did that?"

Jones nodded. "Turns out my allergic reaction had a silver lining. If I hadn't stayed behind, I never would have figured it out. I saw another guest at the lodge put one just like it on her daughter to keep track of her in case she got lost running around in the woods. When I asked the mom about it, she said she bought it at Last Chance General. It connects to an expensive GPS device like this one."

She picked up the unit she'd dropped. "Actually, exactly this one. Her daughter refused to wear the compass, so I was able to convince her to let me borrow this. With a few tweaks, I was able to program it to pick up your signal instead. I suspected I wasn't the only one watching your signal move up Black Bear Mountain. The only reason they would have secretly given you an expensive tracking device and not told you about it is if they were using the GPS unit to monitor you."

"They've been tracking us all over the mountain with that bracelet, just like Dr. K tracks his mountain lions with radio collars!" Frank said.

I pounded my fist into my palm. "It explains how both perps found us so easily. We heard Stinky say 'it jammed' on the radio while we were hiding on the ledge under Aleksei's cave. He must have thought the tracker was frozen, otherwise our trick ruse never would have worked."

"But who are they?" Dr. K asked. "Are Cherry and Ken really involved in this?"

"Cherry's got to be, since she gave the bracelet to Joe, but I don't know about Ken," Jones answered. "I did some more detective work early this morning as soon as I figured it out, and Ken is working alone at the general store today without Cherry. My guess is she never went back to the store after dropping us off."

"Ricky isn't there either," Frank informed her. "He was here helping the Ghost of the Wild Man steal the garnets from us."

"The *ghost*?" Jones asked.

"A guy in a fake beard and a mask with a voice changer to disguise his identity," I explained. "At least he was pretending to be a guy. It could have been Cherry Fritwell in a mask the whole time!"

Dr. K seethed. "I can't believe Cherry or Ken would do this to me. I've been loyal customers of theirs for years."

"Greed can make some people do a lot of things they normally wouldn't," Frank said.

"Cherry was pretty bitter about Aleksei hiding out here all those years, scaring the locals and chasing off business," I added. "That gives her a personal motive, and she could have held it against you for being friends with him and keeping his secret too."

"We also don't know that Ken is in on it," Frank pointed out. "Just because they're husband and wife doesn't mean they're working together."

"Like how Casey didn't know anything about Steven and her sister trying to steal the garnets last time we were here," I said.

"What about Steven? I haven't trusted him ever since," Max said, cracking his knuckles like he was ready for a fight.

"Beard Face wasn't tall enough, but we still haven't gotten a look at Stinky," I said, turning back to Jones. "Stinky is the other perp running around the mountain. We haven't seen him, but we sure have smelled him."

"We have to consider Dan, too. Both he and Cherry had the opportunity to bait our pack with honey. Plus, he's the one who led us to the trap on the ATV ride, and him backing out of guiding us at the last minute is pretty suspicious. He was acting dodgy the whole ride there, too," said Frank.

I mulled it over. "It also could have been either one of

them who stole the letter Dr. K gave to Dan to take to the post office. The post office is *in* the general store, after all."

"Drawes is another wild card. We can't rule him or Dan out as accomplices," Frank added.

"I can," Jones said. "The reason Dan was acting dodgy about ditching you guys is because he went behind the lodge's back and booked a two-day fishing trip with Drawes on the other side of the mountain range. Dan didn't tell Casey or Amina that Drawes booked him because he knew they'd make him cancel to guide you guys. They're both apparently fly-fishing fanatics, and there's some big bug hatch right now that's really good for catching brook trout."

"Tell me about it," I said, smacking another mosquito. "Only I think it's the bugs that are catching *us*."

"We know it's not just a cover story?" Frank asked skeptically.

"Yup. Dan had a guilty conscience about leaving you guys alone after the tree almost took you out. He called in later from his cell phone to tell Amina about it so she could report it to the rangers," Jones explained. "He had cell phone service, so we know he couldn't have been up there on Black Bear Mountain. Amina blew a fuse when she found out. She said Dan will be lucky to still have a job once Casey hears about it. She tried to get him to come right back, but Drawes got on the phone and threw a hissy fit. Said he paid good money for Dan to guide him, and he'd sue if he didn't get his way."

"Sounds like Drawes, all right," Dr. K said.

"Amina tried calling the rangers and the state troopers to report it, but they're all tied up fighting the fire, and all she got was a machine. She tried the local sheriff, too, but they didn't take it seriously. Told her it sounded like kids playing a bad prank. I tried calling the sheriff again after I discovered Cherry was tracking you, but he said I was being paranoid. He said if you still hadn't made it back in two days, I could file a missing persons report and they'd look into it. I wasn't about to wait two days. I know you boys well enough to know the kind of pickles you like to get into."

Frank looked at her with concern. "But you're still recovering! What if you have another allergic reaction?!"

"That's sweet of you to worry about me after everything you guys have just been through, Frank. I know I don't look ready for a night on the town, but I feel all right, really. Almost as good as new." Jones patted her bag. "And I borrowed another epinephrine injector from the lodge just in case. And, um, I kind of borrowed an ATV too. I had to sneak out when poor Amina wasn't looking. This is her first time running the lodge by herself, and between my allergic reaction, you two being in trouble, and Dan playing hooky, she's a total stress ball. When I told her I was going after you, she nearly fainted. She even called Dr. Feigelson and had her scold me. Sneaking out was really my only choice. I never would have taken the chance if I didn't think your lives might depend on it. And I was right!"

"We're safe, thanks to you. Aleksei's garnets aren't,

though," I reminded them. "Cherry Beard Face or whoever's behind that mask is getting away, and we still don't know who he or she radioed or where they're taking the gems. . . . Um, why are you grinning, Frank?"

"I think they gave us a clue before they left. Did you hear what Beard Face said into the radio?"

"It was something like 'on the way to the rendezvous, get ready to go,' I think," Max offered. "But all that tells us is that they're getting away, not where they're going."

"It was garbled, but they definitely said the words 'take off,' not 'ready to go,'" I corrected him, and I started to realize what Frank was getting at as I did.

Max didn't, though. "However they phrased it, of course they're leaving now that they have the demantoids."

"They may have told us more than you realize, Dr. K. Not just *that* they're leaving, but *how* they're leaving. When I first heard it, I assumed they said 'get ready to take off' too, but I couldn't hear the whole thing. What if they didn't say 'get ready *to* take off'—" Frank began to ask.

"What if they said 'get ready *for* takeoff'?" I interrupted to finish the question.

Max gasped as the alternate meaning hit home. "They're flying out!"

"It's just a hunch, but it's the best one we've got," said Frank.

"They could be trying to steal my chopper!" Dr. K exclaimed.

"They'd be trying to get away on a flightless bird if they are. I don't think we're going to get that lucky, though," I said. "We know from how they busted the chopper's radio that they've seen the dismantled control panel, so even if they knew how to fix it *and* how to fly it, they'd still need the part you took."

"The way they've planned everything else out, I'd wager they already had a getaway plan in place when they first came up here," Jones speculated.

"I don't think 'for takeoff' was the only clue they gave us when they radioed their accomplice," Frank said. "Saying 'rendezvous' indicates they're meeting at a pre-arranged destination, and I only picked up fragmented pieces of what they said next, but I definitely heard the word 'way' twice."

I replayed the overheard snippets in my mind, filling in the part we'd already deduced. *Rendezvous time. On . . . way . . . way. Get ready . . . takeoff.* The gap before the first *way* had been really short, and the second one had been a bit longer, like there were a few words missing. I played a quick game of mental *Wheel of Fortune* and started filling in the blanks.

"On the way . . . ," I began, thinking of a destination that matched up with aviation takeoff. The answer clicked right away. "To the runway!"

"That's my guess. We've taken a bush plane up to Black Bear Mountain before; they easily could have too." Frank turned to Dr. K. "Is there another runway besides the one we flew in on last time?"

"That's the only one! Commander Gonzo and the other local pilots maintain the field on the south slope. It's just long enough to get clearance. There's no other safe place up here to land a plane, and if they were flying their own chopper, there are more convenient places to touch down. They've got to have a plane waiting on the south slope!"

"Well, what are we waiting for?" Jones asked. "Let's go after them!"

"With the head start they have, you'll never catch up," Max said, the excitement draining from his voice.

"There's no shortcut?" I asked hopefully, but he just shook his head.

"There's a shortcut to my research station, but not to the south slope. If I had two good legs, we might be able to make it to my chopper in time to intercept them over the runway and keep them from taking off, but in the condition I'm in . . ." He stretched his wounded leg and winced. "It's no use even trying. They'd be halfway across the state before I made it up there."

There was only one word to describe the looks on everyone else's faces. "Defeated." But not mine.

Now it was Frank's turn to ask me the question I'd asked him a few minutes earlier. "Um, why are you grinning, Joe?"

"Grab your stuff, everybody. We're taking that shortcut back to the chopper."

"But without Max, who's going to fly it?"

"You know that helicopter flight simulation game I've been playing?"

"Oh no—"

"I am."

THRILL RIDE

16

FRANK

BUT THAT'S JUST A VIDEO GAME!" I protested.

"A very realistic video game," Joe said confidently.

"Those types of simulation programs *are* similar to what they use to train modern pilots," Dr. K said.

"See, bro? No big deal."

"Yes big deal! We're talking about a real-life helicopter here! Do you remember the last time you tried flying something real?" I asked, reminding him of the high-tech flying car we'd accidentally commandeered on a recent international case in Paris.

"Sure do," he said proudly. "Landed that bad boy without a scratch."

"Yeah, after almost flying us into the Eiffel Tower!"

Joe shrugged. "You said you wanted to do some sightseeing."

"Please tell him this is a bad idea," I pleaded to Dr. K.

"Flying a helicopter isn't easy, even with hands-on training," he said. "I'd be inclined to say no way—"

I sighed with relief. "Thank you, Dr. K—"

Dr. Kroopnik wasn't finished, though. "But I've learned never to doubt a Hardy boy."

I turned to Jones for help. She'd be the voice of reason to talk some sense into them.

"Sorry, Frank, I have to agree with Doc K on that one."

I'm pretty sure my mouth was hanging wide open by this point. Was I the only one with any common sense?

"But the controls are dismantled," I protested. Surely that would dissuade Joe. "You don't know how to fix a helicopter by yourself."

"I can talk you through it easily enough. It's pretty simple to reconnect as long as you have the right part." Dr. Kroopnik pulled out a small fuse.

"See, nothing to worry about, bro-pilot, everything is under control," Joe reassured me unreassuringly. "This is our shot to stop them before they get away."

I closed my eyes and massaged my temples. "I can't believe I'm letting you talk me into this."

"To the chopper!" Joe declared, and started marching up the hill.

"Wait, I still need to tell you how to fix it!" Dr. Kroopnik called after him. "And how to find the shortcut!"

"Right," said Joe, putting on the brakes and turning around. "Got a little overexcited there for a minute."

I buried my face in my hands and groaned. What had I gotten myself into?

For better or worse, we were on our way a few minutes later, helicopter repair instructions and shortcut directions in hand. Jones volunteered to stay and look after Dr. K until we could come back to get them or send for a rescue team. Thankfully, she'd thought to bring a first aid kit with her. We left the compass with the tracking device behind as well so the perps wouldn't see it on the move and know we'd escaped. More important, we took the GPS monitor Jones had brought so we'd know exactly where to find our friends when someone came back to fly them out.

Joe and I booked it back to the chopper, moving as fast as we could without hurting ourselves on the rough terrain. By the time we got there, we were both drenched in sweat and panting from exhaustion. Running up a mountain is no joke! A chance to sit down and rest for a while would have been a relief—if I weren't about to be sitting in a helicopter next to an amateur helicopter pilot who'd never flown before!

Dr. Kroopnik's instructions were spot-on, and when the moment of truth came, the propellers whirred to life just like he said they would.

"This is incredible!" Joe shouted, pumping his fist in the air.

"Incredibly risky!" I squeaked, triple-checking my seat belt.

I'm no stranger to adventure, but gut-dropping voluntary thrill rides like roller coasters, skydiving, high-elevation zip lines, or say, CHASING AFTER AIRPLANES IN HELICOPTERS WITH UNLICENSED FIRST-TIME PILOTS WITH NO FORMAL TRAINING WHATSOEVER? Not so much my jam.

I gripped my seat as tightly as I could and closed my eyes as the small, two-seat helicopter jerked into the air.

"Whoo-hoo!" Joe hollered.

"Ugh," I moaned.

The chopper dipped and lurched clumsily as it rose over the trees. My stomach dipped and lurched along with it. So did my nerves.

"Are you sure you know what you're doing?" I yelled over the sound of the rotors, unable to look.

"More or less," Joe yelled back.

"I'm really rooting for more!"

I felt the aircraft level out as it gained altitude.

"I think I've got the hang of it now!" Joe shouted as the helicopter propelled forward a lot more smoothly than it had been.

I took a deep breath and opened my eyes. The view was spectacular as we zipped over the trees—except for the thick black smoke rising into the sky in the distance to the north where the wildfires were.

"I'm sure glad we're not flying through that," Joe said. "Keep an eye out. The runway should be just over this ridge."

The perps' plane came into view before the runway did. And it wasn't on the ground.

"We're too late!" I yelled as a bush plane rose up from the trees and took to the sky ahead of us.

"Not too late to chase them!" Joe called back.

"That's what I was afraid you'd say!"

The plane was only big enough for a handful of passengers and looked similar to the small Cessna we'd taken last year, but I didn't know enough about the different aircraft manufacturers to tell the difference.

I looked down as we flew over the open field where the makeshift runway was. Two figures looked back up at the helicopter in surprise. One was wearing camouflage. The other was a raccoon. The camouflaged perp had ditched the mask and beard he'd been wearing when he tied us up. He—or should I say she—had also let her hair down. A long braid was draped over her shoulder like it had been at the general store the morning before. The Ghost of the Wild Man was a woman after all.

"It's Cherry and Ricky!" I yelled. "They must have handed the garnets off to Stinky in the plane!"

"Perp One's identity confirmed! Now for Perp Two!" Joe

said, hitting the gas—or whatever it is you hit on a helicopter to make it go faster!

I turned my head to get a last glimpse of Cherry. I couldn't quite tell, but it sure looked like Ricky was shaking his little raccoon fist at us.

The plane rose sharply over the next peak, then took a sudden nosedive over the other side.

"They're trying to shake us!" Joe shouted as the chopper crested the peak. We made it just in time to see the plane's tail disappear down a dangerously narrow canyon wedged between two mountains.

"There it is!" I yelled. Then I saw the look in my brother's eyes as his brain calculated whether or not to follow.

"Joe . . . ," I cautioned him.

"Copy that. As fun as that looks, I think I'll save canyon racing for my second flight," Joe assured me. "As long as we keep a high enough elevation, we should be able to see them come back out."

He was right. The plane rose back over the mountain range a minute later and took a sharp turn north. Straight for the rising cloud of thick black smoke.

"I don't think that canyon dive was his only daredevil move. He's heading straight toward the fire."

"Talk about a smoke screen!" Joe said.

"Talk about reckless! He won't be able to see a thing."

"Neither will we. I think that's the point."

The smoke grew thicker, sweeping over the chopper's

windshield in dark whips as the distance between us and the fire closed. Soon we could see flames leaping from the tree-tops ahead.

"We're losing visibility fast," Joe said, veering the helicopter back toward clean airspace.

I breathed a deep sigh of relief.

"Don't worry, dude," he assured me. "I haven't gotten to this level of the video game yet. Flying blind into a wildfire at low altitude is a little beyond my expertise. That plane is flying barely higher than the mountain peaks, and who knows what he's flying toward."

"We're heading in the direction of town," I said, looking down at the river, which I knew ran past the Bear Foot Lodge toward Last Chance. "Let's keep flying this way on the outskirts of the smoke where we still have visibility and see if he comes back out."

"Good call, bro-pilot. I'm on it."

A skinny metal tower poked into the sky from one of the mountains below.

"There's a cell tower!" I shouted. "I bet that means we have service again."

I reached into our pack, pulled out my phone, and powered it on. Bingo. I dialed only three digits. 9-1-1. It picked up on the first ring.

"There's an emergency rescue situation on Black Bear Mountain," I shouted as loudly as I could, hoping the operator could hear me over the rotors. "Two people are stranded, one of them has a badly injured leg, and the other is recovering from anaphylaxis. They're going to need an airlift out ASAP."

I yelled the coordinates from the GPS tracker into the phone and repeated them twice before clicking off. I was going to tell them about Cherry and our pursuit of Stinky's plane but thought better of it. It sounded so outrageous, I was afraid they'd think the whole call was a hoax.

I studied the GPS, noting the tracking device's location on Black Bear Mountain as well as our position over the next mountain range to the northeast. Smoke blanketed the mountains on Joe's side of the chopper to the my left. Blue skies reached out toward the horizon—and Last Chance—out my door to the right. "We should be due north of town."

Joe scanned the edge of the smoky sky to his left. "The smoke starts to let up ahead. We can swing north and follow the edge of the fire to see if he tries to make a break for it. But if he kept heading north over the thick of it, then we're out of . . ." Joe paused as he squinted out the window. "Look! I think I see the plane!"

The aircraft's silhouette was faint, but sure enough, there it was, flying dangerously low over the mountaintops, veering back toward the clean air ahead of us. That wasn't all it was veering toward, though.

"It's flying straight at that fire tower!" I cried, pointing to the six-story metal-frame tower atop the next mountain peak. It looked a bit like Dr. K's ranger station, only taller.

And it was dead center in the plane's path. "I don't think he can see it!"

"Bank right! Bank right!" Joe screamed out the window, trying to will the pilot to safety.

Whoever was flying that plane had racked up a host of crimes and endangered our lives in his reckless pursuit of Aleksei's garnets, but that didn't mean he deserved to crash. We wanted him brought to justice, not hurt!

We watched helplessly as the distance between the bush plane and the tower closed. I could tell the exact moment the pilot regained visibility—and it was one moment too late. The plane veered sharply to the right as the tower rushed toward it. I held my breath as the fuselage cleared the tower, and for a second I thought he was going to make it. An instant sooner, he would have.

We could hear the impact of the left wing as it took out the fire tower and was ripped from the plane.

FINAL DESCENT

17

JOE

WATCHED IN HORROR AS THE ONE-WINGED plane burst out of the smoke from the wildfire and careened past our windshield, spewing its own trail of smoke behind it. The only thing I could do was follow it as it went down.

"If he bails out, we can still try to rescue him!" Frank shouted.

"Already on it," I said, turning the helicopter south away from the wildfire to stay on the disabled plane's tail.

Frank hit redial on his phone and shouted into it. "There's a bush plane going down south of the forest fire! Get rescue crews—Hello? Hello? Can you hear me?" He looked down at his phone with a grim expression. "I lost the signal."

"The plane's losing altitude fast. He's—" As I looked

ahead, the mountain forest below us started to give way to the first signs of civilization. "Oh no."

The plane was headed straight for Last Chance.

The pilot must have had the same reaction I did, because the plane began struggling to climb. It was still going down fast, but all it would take was a little extra elevation to clear the village before it crashed.

"You can do it!" Frank shouted. "Just a little more!"

"I think it's high enough! As long as he can maintain that trajectory, he can clear the town with room to spare."

"It's all woods on the other side of town. At least no one will get hurt in the crash." Frank paused, watching the smoke billow from the plane's missing wing as the aircraft made its doomed final approach toward Last Chance. "I mean, no one else."

"The pilot!" I shouted, gawking out the windscreen as a lone figure leaped from the plane. "He bailed just in time!"

Relief surged through me as I watched the parachute unfurl over Last Chance.

I didn't have to see the daredevil pilot's face to know who it was. I recognized him instantly.

He floated serenely toward the village as his pilotless plane soared out of control and crashed into the hills on the other side of town. The explosion was almost as bright as his hideously tacky, neon-pink Hawaiian shirt.

LOOK OUT BELOW

18

FRANK

"COMMANDER GONZO!" I SHOUTED AS Last Chance's most eccentric bush pilot parachuted from the burning plane.

How could I be so sure it was him? We'd have to follow him down to the ground to confirm it, but chances were high that a place this remote didn't have more than one wildly reckless, bald-headed, ugly-floral-shirt-wearing pilot.

When we'd flown with him on our last trip, he'd made his introduction by almost crashing a vintage convertible into the side of the Bear Foot Lodge, and then he nearly wrecked the plane before we even took off. Our short flight up to Black Bear Mountain with retired Air Force Flight Commander Gonzo "Doc" Gonzales had certainly been a memorable one. Before flying with Joe, I would have said it had been the most frightening flight of my life. It had also been one of the most entertaining. The guy was totally out there, and he'd been pretty lovable because of it. Apparently, he was also a dangerous gem thief.

"So much for Gonzo being booked on an out-of-state charter," I said.

"Yeah, he was booked, all right," Joe said bitterly. "By Cherry Fritwell."

"Looks like Steven is in the clear. We were suspicious of the wrong out-of-town local."

We'd suspected Steven's out-of-town alibi because he'd already tried to steal the demantoid garnets once before. Gonzo's alibi hadn't raised any red flags because he'd had no connection to the first crime. Sure, his flight safety record may have been suspect, but we'd never had reason to be suspicious of *him*. If anything, he'd been an ally. He'd even taken it on himself to fly back to Black Bear to rescue our stranded friends after we cracked the case.

A jolt of disappointment stabbed me in the gut. Joe and I had worked a lot of cases, and we'd learned that sometimes a person you really like can turn out to be a villain. You never quite got used to it, though. It still hurt every time.

The disappointment was replaced by a wave of relief when the empty plane exploded in the woods safely away from Last Chance. I could see Gonzo salute his lost plane as he floated toward the village.

"I'm going to hover over Main Street and we can follow him if he runs," Joe said. "I've got a few questions for Commander Gonzo."

"I think we're going to get a chance to ask him," I said.

Gonzo had been trying to guide his parachute down toward the pasture next to the cemetery, but Mother Nature had other ideas. A gust of wind caught the chute just as he was approaching the church and carried him straight toward the steeple. He kicked wildly, but it didn't do any good. His body cleared the steeple, but his chute didn't. The chute snagged and ripped—but just far enough to leave Gonzo dangling a story off the ground over the church steps.

Gonzo wasn't running anywhere.

By this time, Joe had the whole helicopter-flying thing down pretty smoothly, and he was able to land safely in the pasture next to the church.

Joe and I stood in front of the little church a minute later, looking up at our dangling, neon-floral-clad perp. He had a cut over his eye, and his yellow-tinted aviator glasses were cockeyed. The skunky odor hadn't worn off any since we'd last smelled him in the cave under Aleksei's cabin.

"Oh, hey, guys. Weird running into you here, huh?" Gonzo called down casually.

"I can say from experience that it's weird running into you anywhere," I told him. "But, yeah, dangling from a church steeple has gotta take the weirdness cake."

"Out of state on a private charter for a few weeks, huh?" Joe asked.

"Just got back an hour ago, would you believe it?" Gonzo replied, making a *go figure* gesture with his hands.

"No. No, we wouldn't," I said.

"Because an hour ago you were waiting to rendezvous with Cherry Fritwell so you could fly away with the garnets she stole before anyone knew you were back in town," Joe said.

"And a few hours before that, you chased us through the secret cave under Aleksei's cabin," I added.

"And a day before that, the tree you rigged by the beaver pond to buy yourself more time to find the garnets almost took out our ATVs," Joe continued.

"And a week before that, you ransacked Dr. Kroopnik's research station," I concluded.

"Who, me?" Gonzo asked, laughing uncomfortably. "Where in the world did you get that wacky idea?"

I glared up at him. "You mean besides the fact that we just saw you leave Cherry on Black Bear right after she shot at us, tied us up, and stole the garnets, and then flew your plane into a wildfire to try to get away from us when we chased you?"

"Yeah, besides that," he insisted, as if all the evidence we'd just laid out for him was somehow inclusive.

"Your cologne," Joe informed him. "Eau de Skunk. We can smell you from down here."

"Just like we smelled you in the cave," I said.

"And smelled the skunk that sprayed you in Dr. Kroopnik's research station," Joe said.

"Your denial stinks as much as you do," I said.

He took a curious sniff of his own shirt. "Ya know, the smell grows on you after a while. I kinda like it."

"Hand over the garnets, Gonzo," I demanded.

"What garnets?" he asked with what was supposed to pass for a confused look.

Joe and I both sighed. He was as stubborn as he was quirky.

"We caught you neon-pink-handed, Gonzo," Joe said. "Lying about it isn't going to do you any good when the cops cut you down and find them on you anyway."

"Your plane isn't the only thing going down for this, and the authorities will go a lot easier on you if you cooperate," I said.

Now it was Gonzo's turn to sigh, only his sounded like resignation. "I told them we should have called it off when Cherry radioed to tell me you boys were coming. She figured we weren't going to get a better chance to search the mountain with the rangers and troopers all tied up fighting the fire."

"Talk about an effective diversion," I said. "The fire's the reason they couldn't send anyone to check on Dr. K when we called from Bayport. Jones and Amina couldn't even get through to report the trap you set for us at the beaver dam."

"Oh, Cherry's aces at planning a heist. She'd been reading Kroopnik's mail at the post office before sending it out for months too. Reading his letters is how she figured out the rumors about the garnets still being hidden up there were true. Then she tried to create a rift between the friends and stopped sending his letters. That way, she figured Aleksei would blame Kroopnik when the garnets disappeared."

"Funny, it's exactly because Aleksei expected a letter and didn't get one that he wrote to us and asked us to investigate," I said. "Cherry's scheming to avoid suspicion is actually what put us on the case."

"I told her you boys were good. Shoulda trusted my instincts after seeing how you foiled the last dupes who tried stealing these things."

Gonzo pulled the plastic bag with the demantoids from the breast pocket of his Hawaiian shirt and gave the gems a last wistful look. "Shine on, you sparkly garnets. Wish I coulda gotten to know ya better."

He tossed the bag down to us and gave it a sad wave as it fell to the ground. Sunlight caught the gems when I lifted the bag, sending a rainbow of prismatic sparkles dancing over us. They were just as beautiful every time I saw them.

I looked back up at Gonzo. I still couldn't help liking the kooky guy, even after everything he had pulled.

"We saw how you steered the plane away from town to keep anyone else from getting hurt in the crash. We'll make sure to let the authorities know your actions helped avoid more casualties, in case it makes a difference."

Gonzo grinned. "Was some pretty fancy flying, if I do say so myself. One-winged birds don't like to fly where you tell them." The grin disappeared as he bit down on his lip. "Never did mean for anyone to get hurt. Just wanted some adventure and a little extra money in my pocket is all."

"You're kind of forgetting the part where you tried to kill us with a tree," Joe reminded him.

"That was Cherry's idea for me to hike back down and do that. I figured it would just scare you a bit and slow you down. Didn't think it would actually hurt you."

I looked at the plume of smoke rising from the hill where Gonzo's plane had crashed. "Gonzo, has anyone ever told you that you have really questionable judgment?"

"Sure! My CO in the air force used to tell me that all the time! That was a pretty impressive wipeout, though, wasn't it? I haven't crashed in years. Forgot how much I enjoy it!"

Gonzo looked genuinely enthusiastic even though he was about to go to jail for criminal conspiracy, assault, and grand larceny, to name just a few of the charges he'd racked up. You had to hand it to the guy for finding the silver lining.

"This caper was nothing personal against Kroopnik or that gangster guy, Orlov. Heck, I admire the big fellow for pulling that wild hermit stunt and living up there all those years. Now there's a man who knew how to crash a plane!" Gonzo gave the air a little salute. "Nah,

I just signed on for the payday. It was them who had the grudge."

"Them?" I asked. We'd been so caught up in questioning Gonzo, we'd forgotten about the possibility of him and Cherry having more accomplices.

"Yeah, Cherry and him." He gestured across the street toward the general store and waved. "Hey, Ken!"

We turned to see Ken Fritwell parked out front in a beat-up old pickup truck, frantically trying to get the engine to turn over. He looked up at the sound of Gonzo calling his name. The look on his face when he saw us is best described by one word: "panic."

CHERRY BOMB

19

JOE

"DON'T GO ANYWHERE," I CALLED UP TO Gonzo as Frank and I sprinted across the street toward Ken Fritwell's stalled pickup truck.

"Take your time, boys," Gonzo called back. "I'll just hang out here."

We were halfway across the street when Ken gave up trying to start the pickup and flung open the door to run. Unfortunately for him, he was still wearing his seat belt.

"Oomph!" he grunted as the seat belt jerked him back into place.

I kicked the driver's-side door closed to make sure he didn't get a second chance.

"Going somewhere, Ken?" I asked through the open

window as Frank leaped over the hood to stand guard at the passenger-side door.

He gave a dismayed look from Frank to me to Gonzo dangling from the church behind me, then opened and closed his mouth a couple of times before answering. "I—I want to talk to my lawyer."

The two-way radio lying on the seat next to him crackled to life.

"Where are you, Ken?" Cherry's angry, undisguised voice shouted from the receiver.

Ken tried to grab it, but Frank was quicker, reaching through the window to snatch it off the seat.

"Ken?" Cherry's voice continued to shout. "Did you get the go bags and our cash from the safe? I'm hiking down to the van. You'd better be waiting when Ricky and I get there. I'm not going to jail because you took your sweet time packing."

"Hiya, Cherry," Frank said cheerily into the two-way. "I think Ken is going to be a little late."

There was a loud burst of static and unintelligible yelling. It did not sound happy.

Frank hit the talk button again. "I'm guessing he radioed to tell you about Gonzo's church visit? Did he mention that we got back the garnets you stole too?"

"I didn't steal anything! Those are ours!" she screamed over the radio.

I came around to the other side of the truck and took the two-way from Frank. "Actually, they're Aleksei Orlov's, and we plan on returning them to him," I said. That didn't make Cherry too happy.

"Orlov's a thieving con. He just stole them from someone else anyway. We have just as much right to those gems as he does. More! These are our mountains! We've been here our whole lives. That imposter was squatting in our backyard, running around scaring people. Scaring away *business*. Any stolen loot that criminal left behind should be ours!"

We'd known Cherry was bitter about Aleksei hiding out in the woods perpetuating the old Wild Man legend. I just hadn't realized how bitter. She also happened to have her facts mixed up.

"You're wrong, Cherry," Frank corrected her. "Aleksei is the first person to admit he stole money from people years ago in his mobster days, and he's paying the legal price for those crimes in prison now. But he brought those demantoid garnets with him all the way from his childhood home in Siberia. They're rightfully his, and he's been donating the proceeds from selling them to charity to help make up for what he did wrong."

"I didn't see him offering to pay us back for all the tourism business his cannibal act cost us," she snapped. "No way some thieving outsider should be living rich in our backyard while us locals are struggling to keep our lights on."

Truth was, she kind of had a point. Not about living

rich, but I don't think we or Aleksei had thought enough about how his actions had impacted the local community. I also knew Aleksei well enough to know it was something he would take responsibility for and want to make right when he got out and returned to Black Bear Mountain. There were ways to right a wrong, and Cherry's wasn't one of them.

"Turning around and hurting other people doesn't make you any less of a criminal than you're accusing Aleksei of being. Dr. Kroopnik, Jones, Frank, and I all could have been seriously injured, or worse."

"The best thing you can do now to help your case is cooperate and bring yourself in," Frank said into the two-way.

Cherry's voice was just as angry as before. "These are our mountains, and you're all trespassers as far as I'm concerned. Especially Kroopnik. He knew for years that mobster was living there, and he helped him. He had it coming to him."

I looked at Frank and shook my head. Cherry's greed and anger had blinded her to reason. We weren't going to be able to talk sense into her no matter how hard we tried.

"We've got all the evidence we need already, Cherry," I said into the two-way. "We'll let the police finish this discussion when they pick you up."

The radio went silent. Cherry was gone.

"My Cherry can have a bit of a temper," Ken said meekly, volunteering to speak for the first time.

"You think?" I asked.

"Sure, she can get a little carried away sometimes, but you don't know what it's been like for us. I can't say whether it's your friend Orlov's fault, but this town's been struggling for a long time. Sure, business has picked up since all the press his story got last time you were here. We might even be doing okay if it weren't for all the debt we racked up trying to keep the store open during the lean years. Heck, I can't even afford to get a pickup that starts when you turn the key." Ken gave a forlorn laugh.

"This store has been in my family since Last Chance was built. I didn't want to lose it. So when Cherry suggested we go find the garnets for ourselves, it seemed like a reasonable idea. One of these so-called treasure hunters who've been running around might have found them if we hadn't anyway. Why shouldn't it be us? I didn't want some weekend warrior from the city getting rich off our mountains while we sat back and watched."

"You weren't just trying to find some random lost treasure, you were trying to take it away from the people who rightfully had it," Frank said. "Max Kroopnik isn't a weekend warrior from the city. He lives here, and he's your customer."

"At least he *was* your customer," I pointed out. "I don't think he'll be giving you much business after this."

Ken looked guiltily down at his lap. "Cherry didn't mean it about Max deserving it. We didn't want anyone to get hurt. We were just going to spy on Max and get him to lead us to the gems. And then when we found out you were coming, we figured we'd just try to scare you away and buy some more time."

"By crushing us with a tree?" I asked.

Ken winced. "I didn't know about that until after. Cherry told Gonzo to slow you down, and well, the Commander's ideas tend to be a little more enthusiastic than well thought out."

"Yeah, we kinda noticed that," Frank said. Gonzo was the same guy who'd thought it was a good idea to fly blindly into a cloud of wildfire smoke at low altitude.

We looked back up across the street at Ken's accomplice, who seemed to be dangling contentedly from the steeple, picking his teeth with a toothpick.

"All I did was stick some honey in one of your packs when I put them in the van," Ken confessed. "That's not so bad, right? Just a harmless little prank."

I think I actually growled. All that lost gear had been a royal pain in our everywhere.

"There's a very well-supplied bear that owes you a thank-you note," Frank said.

"I'm sorry if we caused any harm." Ken stared up at the painted sign above his store. "This was our chance to score big and really get the store back on its feet. This was the last chance for Last Chance General."

"I'm sorry about your store, Ken," I said, genuinely meaning it. "This just wasn't the way to save it."

"I'm sorry about this, too," Frank said, reaching down and picking a length of cord off the messy truck floor. "But we're going to have to restrain you until the police get here."

Ken nodded sadly and let us tie his hands to the steering wheel. We were careful to make sure the cord wasn't too tight.

I hadn't noticed until we'd run across the street to Ken's pickup truck, but we had attracted a crowd. A man jumping out of a fiery plane onto the church roof and a helicopter landing on Main Street will do that.

The excitement wasn't over, either. A larger, bright red helicopter with the words SEARCH AND RESCUE emblazoned on the doors swept over town and landed in the street.

A woman in a matching red jumpsuit leaped out of the cockpit. "We got the 'plane down' call. Is anyone hurt?"

"Everyone's okay!" Frank called out.

"Even him?" she asked, pointing up at Gonzo, who waved.

"Even him," I said. "Fly boy and his accomplice in the pickup can skip the hospital and go straight to jail."

"Are these the ones responsible for assaulting the folks in that other rescue call we got on Black Bear Mountain?" she asked.

"That's them," I confirmed. "They've got an armed accomplice named Cherry Fritwell who is fleeing the mountain on foot now if you want to call it in to the police."

"Frank!" a familiar friendly voice called from the open helicopter doors.

"Jones!" Frank cried.

She jumped down from the helicopter and ran over to hug Frank and me. "I'm so glad you guys are okay. We were in the search-and-rescue chopper on our way to the hospital when they got the call about an aircraft going down. Max and I were scared something had happened to you."

"Something did," said Frank, smiling. "We caught the rest of the bad guys."

"It looks like the church caught that one," Jones said, looking up at Gonzo. "That's the charter pilot from the poster at the general store."

"Aka Stinky," I said. "Cherry and Ken recruited him."

"So it was the three of them?" Jones asked.

"Four if you count Ricky," Frank said. "Do you think they put raccoons in jail?"

"If there's ever a raccoon that deserves it, it's him," I declared.

"How is Dr. Kroopnik holding up?" asked Frank.

"Good enough that we were able to talk the pilot into putting off the hospital and diverting the chopper to help here instead," Jones replied.

"Good thing you did, because we've got something to return to him," Frank said, patting his pocket.

Dr. Kroopnik waved eagerly from the back of the search-and-rescue chopper as we headed over. "I can't tell you how happy I am to see you boys are still complete specimens."

"You'll be even happier when you see what we brought you," I said.

Frank pulled the bag with the dazzling green garnets from his pocket and handed them to Dr. Kroopnik.

"This time, these beauties are going straight into my safe-deposit box until Aleksei gets back," he said, studying the gems as if for the first time. "Next time you all come to visit, let's try to keep the outdoor activities to hiking and camping. I think I've had enough of the assault, kidnapping, and jewel theft!"

Frank held out his hand so they could shake on it. "Deal!"

"You found them!" a voice shouted from the crowd of onlookers as Dr. Kroopnik temporarily returned the garnets to his own pocket. When I turned around, I saw a tall, buff guy with a camouflage military jacket and a buzz cut. The description clicked right away. It did for Frank, too.

"John Smith," he said.

"Hey, how'd you know my name?" the man asked. His hand went reflexively to the chain around his neck, and I could see that he was wearing military-issue dog tags. The surprise on his face looked genuine.

"Huh, so John Smith actually is your real name," I surmised. "We had it pegged as an alias."

"Of course it's my real name," he barked, holding up the dog tags for us to see. "What's going on here? How do you know who I am?"

"We did a little asking around at the Bear Foot Lodge to figure out who might have been causing problems for Dr. Kroopnik," Frank replied.

"Dr. who?" Smith asked.

"My research isn't quite that advanced," Dr. K replied with an amused smile.

By this point, Smith looked entirely baffled. He clearly didn't know who Dr. K was or what he was talking about. He squinted from the four of us by the rescue chopper over to Gonzo dangling from the church steeple and scratched his head. It was pretty obvious he'd been a false lead and wasn't involved in the Fritwell-Gonzo heist conspiracy. If he had been, he wouldn't have hung around looking dumbfounded while the rescue pilot radioed for police backup from a few feet away.

"All that time wandering around the mountain without finding anything, and some kids beat me to the treasure." He shook his head in resignation. "From the looks of things, you earned it with whatever ordeal you went through."

"Black Bear Mountain never disappoints in the adventure department, that's for sure," I said.

"Beaten by teenagers . . ." John Smith sighed and walked off muttering to himself.

Sirens pierced the mountain air as a pair of police cars sped down Main Street and screeched to a stop in front of the Last Chance General Store.

"Late as usual," I said.

Last Chance and Bayport were about as different as two towns could get—except for one thing: the police usually didn't show up until after the Hardy boys had already solved the crime.